THE TIMES OF INDIA

THE MIDDLES KINGDOM

UNCOMMON WRITINGS OF THE COMMON MAN

Times Group Books

Middle Stories

by

Bennett, Coleman & Co. Ltd.
7, Bahadur Shah Zafar Marg
New Delhi-110 002

Design & distribution : Times Group Books
Printed and bound by : Brijbasi Art Press Limited

ISBN 978-81-89906-46-7
Price : Rs.150

CONTENTS

PREFACE

NOT EVERYTHING PUBLISHED in a newspaper has the brief shelf life of greengrocery. Sometimes an article or a piece under a column transcends the perishable character of topical news, earning a degree of literary immortality. The Middle in *The Times of India*, which had a run of more than 60 years, was a column that harvested such sparkling gems.

The Middle began appearing in the 1950s or perhaps even earlier than that and it remained a 'fiercely sought after space' until 2004 when ironically 'enormous pressure on space' crowded it out, making the column a historic relic on the yellowing pages of TOI.

The Middle earned its name simply because it appeared on the middle of the page. While some called it Middle Story others referred to it as just Middle. The column came to acquire in course of time many virtues such as a rich history, an array of distinguished contributors and a plethora of themes. It became an instant hit, so much so that many avid readers opened first of all the edit page and delved straightaway into the Middle. No other column in any daily had such a devoted following.

Soon after the Middle made its first appearance it had many readers hooked. From a *babu* to a civil servant, from a housewife to a college student, and from a top business executive to a lowly assistant, they all savoured the Middle with delight. They in fact looked forward to the piece with much eagerness every morning.

Some of the readers even contributed to the column. The passion for Middle spawned readers clubs across different regions, age groups and professions. People who founded these clubs sometimes wrote Middles in response to others' Middles. Raj Chatterjee, a contributor to the column for six decades, became a sort of a legend in his own lifetime. Jug Suraiya, who for years selected from among an overflowing crop of contributions to

Middles for publication recalls how much he was harried by the Middle writers even as he was in the thick of work, dealing with weightier matter of the editorial page. Middlemania was phenomenal indeed.

The collection in this book brings to readers some of the best Middles. While most of them are reminiscences of old times, some reflect on life in the defence services and some others are purely humorous pieces. A few of them have a didactic ring about them. A common thread that runs through all of them is their all time readability and their unfailing ability to delight.

WIRELESS WRANGLES

TANUSHREE PODDER

ALTHOUGH WE HAVE been married for many years now, I can count the number of wedding anniversaries we have spent together. In fact, we have stayed together for only 50 per cent of our married life. That, of course, has some advantages. We still think of ourselves as a newly-married couple. I have had to console myself on most anniversaries by celebrating it with a few close friends sans the valiant half, who is generally posted away, either fighting militants in the Valley or locked in combat somewhere in the North-East.

After a stint of about four years in the Valley and the East, he was finally posted to a peace station and I joined him there. I was quite happy at the idea of having him around for the birthdays and our marriage anniversary. I decided to have a large bash for the anniversary. Come November, and I was excitedly preparing to throw a party for the officers of the regiment and their families. At the eleventh hour the hubby was sent away on a firing exercise to the ranges. An army wife learns to take these things in her stride. However, I managed to extricate a promise from him — that he would call me up and speak to me from whichever location he was at.

On the precious day, the phone rang even as I was preparing the breakfast. He hadn't forgotten, my heart sang with a romantic tremor. The operator informed me that the Tiger (Commanding

Officer) was trying to contact me through the wireless radio set. The code was 'Alpha 2' and I should say 'over' at the end of each statement, I was instructed.

The conversation went something like this: "Calling Alpha 2, Alpha 2 comes in. Over."

The receiver crackled and the metallic voice of my spouse rode the distance: "Alpha 2 here. Many happy returns of the day, darling. Over." In my excitement I had already begun to speak, forgetting that it was a one-way communication and he couldn't hear me till the 'over' was said and he had switched the buttons.

"Ditto, ditto. Happy anniversary and I love you," I replied, waiting for his response. My inexperienced self had forgotten to add the ever important 'over'. I waited for a few moments before realizing it and shouted back, 'over', after a brief lull.

Prompt came the reply: "I ... " and the voice went faint. I couldn't hear anything except the sound of my own breathing.

Frustrated, I called out, "Alpha 2 come in, come in Alpha 2. What is it you were saying?"

After a brief hesitation, the helpful operator was back on the line, "*Madam, Tiger ne ILU bola*. Over." Mad at the outrageous situation, I shouted back, "Why the hell are you butting in? Get lost. To hell with everything. Over."

The line connected suddenly and the wires crackled back into life. "Roger. Same to you with my compliments. Alpha 2 signing out. Over and out," came the furiously simmering comment from my hubby. And the radio went dead. I don't know whether it was my imagination, but I suspect I heard something like a chuckle.

THE SOUND OF MUSIC

CV ARVIND

IT WAS MY first night in Patna and the cold was at its worst. Wrapping a thick blanket around my thin frame I had retired to bed hoping that sleep would soon overtake me. It did. Hardly had I shut my eyes when a loud, guttural voice shattered the stillness of the night. For the next one hour I had to endure the cacophony, trapped as I was within my one-room apartment. It was only after the merciless onslaught on my aural nerves ceased that I could scamper back to bed. But the voice continued to ring in my ears making it almost impossible for me to snatch some sleep.

From the direction of the sound I guessed that it was my landlord's wife or daughter doing her *sadhana* (music practice to the uninitiated). Therefore, broaching the subject would be rather delicate, more so because I had got this accommodation after searching high and low, traversing the dirty streets of the capital of Bihar, or Lalooland as it is more popularly known now.

Further it would have been highly indecent on my part to rush up the stairs, knock on my landlord's door and ask him to ensure that whoever owned that blessed larynx should pipe down immediately. We South Indians are well known in the north as confirmed masochists who would offer the other cheek for a resounding slap without a moment's hesitation. And, I had to live up to that reputation, appalling as the prospect was. Hoping that good sense would dawn on whosoever had created that din, I went off to work and returned late at night and went straight to bed.

The clock struck 11 and the ordeal began. The sound of music came filtering through my firmly-closed windows, beating a tattoo on my eardrums. As it reached an alto, I could feel my temples pounding, my BP soaring and my heart sinking, thinking of the nights ahead. Days passed without respite and my patience was wearing thin. Then came the last straw — the 'solo' turned into a 'duet' with the new voice matching the old in terms of sheer shrillness and pitch. The music buff in me rebelled and I put on one of my favourite Lata Mangeshkar numbers on my two-in-one. But, alas, poor Lata didn't stand a chance. Her dulcet voice was drowned in no time. It was a hopeless situation.

A month passed. I went up to pay the rent and gently informed my landlady that they were ruining my sleep. "Would it be possible for you and your daughter to sing before supper?" I enquired. The lady looked at me from head to toe as a butcher would a goat that he wanted to buy, and let out a loud guffaw that sent a hundred centipedes crawling down my bony back. Her next sentence almost brought about a collapse. "My dear man," she began, "when you took up your lodging here, my husband informed me that you had great interest in music. So we were just entertaining you night after night." My face fell. I mumbled an apology and left.

THE REASON WHY

RAJ CHATTERJEE

I HAVE OFTEN wondered why I have failed to make my mark in the literary world with a novel or two on contemporary life, splashed with a sufficient number of four-letter words to qualify for the Booker Prize. And now I think I have found the answer — in an old copy of *Time* which fell out of a cupboard in the house, where we keep odds and ends.

Reading an article in this, it seemed that the cause of my failure to hit the jackpot is that I don't hit the bottle hard enough. I don't have what the *Time* article calls the 'writer's vice'. This particular writer's thesis was based on the findings of a Washington University psychiatrist, Donald Goodwin. With the American obsession for statistics, Prof. Goodwin had discovered that in the present century a third to a half of the best-known American writers have been alcoholics.

Further, that of the six Americans awarded the Nobel Prize for Literature, four — Eugene O'Neill, Sinclair Lewis, William Faulkner and Ernest Hemingway — were compulsive drinkers while a fifth, John Steinbeck, was not far behind. This leaves only Pearl Buck, of whom the Prof makes no mention.

The Prof's reasoning seems plausible enough. Writing, he said, is a form of exhibitionism. It requires an interest in people; alcohol increases sociability. It involves fantasy; alcohol promotes fantasy. It requires self-confidence; alcohol bolsters self-confidence. He might have added that to someone with a limited vocabulary writing is a headache and that an excessive use of alcohol provides this quite easily.

Indeed, one is led to believe that in order to become a money-spinning author one must earn some form of notoriety. But, the sort of notoriety that sent Oscar Wilde to Reading Gaol would not rate him for the briefest mention in today's newspapers. Incidentally, Wilde was no match for the Nobel Prize-winners mentioned by Prof Goodwin. In fact, on the subject of drink, he stopped being witty and was merely stupid. "I have made an important discovery," he once said, "that alcohol taken in sufficient quantities, produces all the effects of intoxication." We call it a hangover these days!

But the vices acquired by writers are not all of a kind that may be considered reprehensible by our prissy, bourgeois standards of morality. George Bernard Shaw, for instance, carried on a long love affair with the celebrated actress, Mrs Patrick Campbell, by a mere exchange of letters. And when the dancer, Isadora Duncan, suggested to GBS that a child produced by the two of them would be a genius with his brains and her beauty, he asked what would happen if the child inherited his face and her brains!

Sometimes, harmless 1 have proved adequate to add lustre to an already famous name. Dr Johnson was a glutton. George Sand, whose real name was Armandine Lucille Aurore, went about dressed as a man. Kipling used to attend, in summer, the office of the Civil and Military Gazette clad in a pair of cotton trousers and a thin vest, a sartorial combination that no newspaper editor would attempt even during a day-long power cut!

CHALO JHUMRITILAIYA

ASEEM K JHA

THE FACT THAT there is much in a name dawned on me when I came to Delhi to join the all-pervasive empire of babudom. My boss was flabbergasted when I disclosed, somewhat sheepishly, that I hailed from Jhumritilaiya (JT). He couldn't believe that there really existed a place by that name on this planet. Even my new colleagues and sundry others looked at me as if I had descended from Timbuctoo. For them JT was only an imaginary land a la Malgudi.

Located in the sylvan dale of Damodar in the Chhotanagpur plateau of Bihar, the place derives its name from *jhoom rahi talaiya* (the lake is swaying) as a beauteous lake abuts on it. It is about 20km from Tilaiya Dam where the first hydro-electric power project of independent India was inaugurated by Pandit Nehru in the early 1950s. JT started gaining popularity among the hoi polloi in the 1960s when the Vividh Bharati programme was started by AIR to counter the appeal of Sri Lanka Broadcasting Corporation.

That was the golden age of radio. These two broadcasting organizations vied with each other for popularity by airing a plethora of *farmaishi* programmes and hit parades of Hindi film songs. A deluge of request-letters from JT were mailed to these programmes. Even in today's channel-surfing era, my ears sometime resonate with the voice of some compere of the bygone days... "*aur Jhumritilaiya se Ganga Prasad Magadhia.*" GPM ran a humble shoe shop in the town and he regularly sent his *farmaish* for perennial hits like, *Awaz de kahan hai, Jab dil hi toot gaya* etc. With the passage of time the name of this abracadabra-sounding place got stuck in the minds of people. Subsequently it attracted the imagination of Bollywood script and song writers too. In umpteen potboilers churned out from Bollywood, macho hero shouts at the villain, *maar maar ke Jhumritilaiya pahuncha doonga* while the nymphet heroine does double-entendre gymnastics to the tunes of *Jhumritilaiya mein paani ki tanki.*

Jhumritilaiyawallahs are connoisseurs of good food. The place is famous for its delicious *kalakand.* And its idli and dosa are tastier than what you get in any downtown restaurant even in southern India. A large chunk of the population is Punjabi. And if Punjabis are there *chhole-bhature* can't be far behind. Jhumritilaiya is the largest producer of mica in India. Even as you enter the periphery of the town you'll be dazzled by the glittering mica refuse-dumps littered on either side of the road.

It's another matter that the mineral has lost much of its lustre in international commerce. The importance of JT can be gauged from the fact that even the prestigious Howrah Rajdhani has a scheduled halt here. I still remember the day when the Rajdhani had stopped there for the first time. All the passengers were greeted with sweets and bouquets. If you plan to visit JT, book a ticket for Koderma. There doesn't exist a railway station by JT's name, even though the platform lies in the heart of the town. That is the mystery and enigma of Jhumritilaiya.

STING OF THE NIGHT

CARMEN FERNANDES

ONE SEPTEMBER NIGHT a total stranger, *P Falciparum*, turned my whole world North-Pole-down. I woke up with my entire body writhing in pain; my head seemed like it would explode. But the time-bomb just kept ticking away, unfortunately each tick was like a Mike Tyson blow to my cranial punching bag. My doctor gave me a shot, tablets were gulped down, an intravenous followed and then all hell broke loose.

I guess Fal had decided that tormenting my body wasn't torture enough, my mind needed to be attacked as well. So, somewhere in distance, I could hear my doctor say, "You must remain conscious; don't let sleep overcome you." I heard him through an aural fog and knew he meant business. This was when harsh realization dawned on me that I was fighting for my life!

Unconsciousness was like a whirlpool, pulling me down into its dangerous depths. And then I saw myself trying to focus my thinking. It was like a kaleidoscope with the imagery changing every few seconds: Why did I take it upon myself to teach my son certain subjects? I should have sent him for tuition classes like most other kids. Will my husband be shattered or, given time, will he pick up the threads of life again? Will my 86-year-old mother withstand the shock and like the Rock of Gibraltar stand by my husband and son? Will He let me through the Pearly Gates? Would my friends at work miss me like I'd miss them? A week before my illness, my boss had lost a friend, and he travelled from Mumbai to

Pune for the funeral. When he returned, I asked him if he was okay, and he said, "I don't let these things disturb me. Life has to go on." So, I knew that 'this thing' would certainly not disturb him! And then, I thought of Stephen Covey, who in his book, *Seven Habits of Highly Effective People*, had said that you should visualize your tombstone to know what the world thinks of you. And I wondered which of the two tombstones would be chosen, because I love to talk and was trying hard to curtail this habit: "Here lies Carmen; Silent at Last!" or "Here lies Carmen; Quiet as Usual."

By this time, I had lost control over my limbs; my hands refused to reach out to touch the people I loved; my tongue weighed a tonne and my speech slurred. But poor Fal failed to totally dominate my mind, and so my thoughts kept me alive; thoughts which I forced myself to think to keep from falling prey to Fal.

It was then, in the deepening haze, I heard the doctor say that now I could sleep if I wanted to — and I knew I had won. Is this what mind over matter means? I knew I would see my family and friends when, and not if, I woke up the next morning. O Malaria! Where is thy sting?

TO SIR WITH RESPECT

SURAJIT DAS

MA ZAFFAR was my mathematics teacher in class VI way back in the late '50s. Mr Zaffar was one of the few lay teachers who taught at my English medium school run by white missionaries. He was a refugee from Bihar who had fled to Chittagong in erstwhile East Pakistan to escape from the communal riots in Bihar during Partition. Having suffered so much from Hindu *goondas*, you would have thought that he would nurse a grievance against us Hindus and thus dislike the hateful Hindus who had made him leave his home in Bihar. But I say this to his credit: That he empathically and emphatically understood the plight of the frightened minority community surrounded by a hostile majority; whether the minority was Hindu or Muslim was immaterial to him.

One incident will reveal his innate predisposition to protect a member of the minority community, the underdog, against a member of the bullying majority community though the latter happened to share his religion, his language and his state of origin. I was one of the very few Hindu students in my class, the majority being Muslims, not from Bengal but from UP, Bihar, Hyderabad, Punjab even Baluchistan.

One day as we were leaving the classroom and going down the staircase, a Muslim boy whose mother tongue was Urdu (he was a refugee from Bihar) brutally told me, "Why are you here? This is Pakistan, meant only for Muslims like us. No place for you here. Why don't you go to India? You belong there, not here." I did not reply to that boy but I became very upset and tears streamed down my face. The boy left immediately after delivering this ultimatum. Moments later, Mr Zaffar overtook me in the staircase and seeing me in tears, asked what the matter was. Initially, I refused to disclose what had happened. But when he persisted I had to reveal all that that bully of a boy had hurled at me. Mr Zaffar looked concerned and told me reassuringly not to worry as he would soon speak to the boy.

What Mr Zaffar told that boy I do not know. But whatever he had told him was effective. The boy no longer repeated those hurtful and hateful words to me. In fact, he avoided me sullenly.

I was grateful to Mr Zaffar. That a Muslim adult, despite his suffering at the hands of Hindus, should come forward to protect a Hindu boy from humiliation and rejection showed that the communal virus did not affect a common Muslim like him. Mr Zaffar and I shared a common fate — of belonging to the minority community, he in India and I in Pakistan. I owe my freedom from communal hatred to Mr Zaffar's example. He showed me how to be free from it. It is more than a commitment to an abstract idea. Zaffar sir, with due respect, more than the mathematics you taught me, it is only this lesson that I have not forgotten to this day.

LUNCH IS REDDY

KRISHAN KALRA

MANY A FAUX pas is caused by the multiplicity of languages in our great land. Serious 'misunderstandings' have arisen at times. However, such situations provide hilarious interludes in the otherwise rule-bound life of our 'twice born' bureaucrats. One such instance was recently narrated by a distinguished retired member of this fraternity. Four decades back, our friend was posted as an assistant collector in a subdivision in Tamil Nadu. The state governor was visiting the district to inaugurate two projects — an overhead water tank in the municipal park and a new maternity ward in the local hospital. Although the first lady had picked up a little Tamil — probably from the Raj Bhavan staff — His Excellency didn't understand a word of this rich language.

When he was invited to speak at the first venue, the Hon'ble Governor promptly took out a folded paper from his sherwani pocket — he had assiduously refused the assistant collector's offer to give him the speeches one by one — and started waxing eloquent about the great need for good pre- and post-natal care of the poor in the state. Those in the audience, who understood English, were in splits. The governor's wife who had seen some Tamil banners and knew they were in the park, too was aghast. She wanted to restrain her husband. Repeated tugs on the sherwani only got polite, dismissive slaps on her hand.

With "Don't disturb me" writ large on his face, the VVIP went on praising the good doctors and devoted missionary nurses..., till his secretary pointed out the mistake and requested him to take out the other speech. All this time, the Tamil translator — who had understood the mix-up — merrily kept on reading out translation of the appropriate speech. So the non-English-speaking audience never really caught on. Now the entourage was at the other site.

Before going on the stage, there was a cake to be cut and a line-up of hospital staff to be introduced. The poor assistant collector had been forewarned by the first lady that Excellency suffered from acute diabetes but was also an obsessive eater. It was his brief to ensure that the great man didn't eat too much. For the young officer, it was a test. Our friend quietly removed the ribboned knife and told the governor that the cake was only symbolic and didn't need to be cut.

"Never mind," said our good man and promptly took out a small knife from his cavernous pocket. Before anyone could say "Congratulations," he had carved out a big piece and stuffed it into his salivating mouth. And now the embarrassed young officer was introducing the hospital staff, "Narayan Rao, Venkata Naidu, Nanji Guruswami..." The governor would graciously repeat the name and shake hands with each one. "Laxman Reddy," said the man.

"Lunch is ready, did you say?" interjected the governor. "Very good, let's go," and he started walking briskly towards the *pandal.*

ROYAL PHYSICIAN

VN KAKAR

ANYONE UNDER THE influence of some ominous star? Anyone on whom has fallen the shadow of a woman that has produced a still-born babe? Anyone who has been cursed by a *kaljibi* (woman with a black tongue whose curses had devastating effects)? Anyone on whom someone has cast an evil eye? Call Bhai Nathu Singh. He had a cure for all kinds of mysterious diseases.

Men and women apart, Bhai Nathu Singh had a cure for houses, too. Houses that were infested with ghosts. Houses from which strange frightening sounds came at the dead of the night. Bhai Nathu Singh had two kinds of treatment. He would subject his patient — man, woman or house — to a recitation of his mantras. Then would come his famous *pudiya* (powder wrapped in paper). Human beings had to swallow the powder with milk. Houses had to absorb it in all their nooks and corners.

Bhai Nathu Singh's treatment was always considered to be highly efficacious. People from all over Peshawar used to flock to him. They came not just for those mysterious diseases but also for conventional ones like ache in the head or pain in the stomach. Bhai Nathu Singh's big, black, oblong pills were considered to be particularly effective in controlling cholera. Every Kumbh mela, Bhai Nathu Singh used to go all the way from Peshawar to Hardwar. Not just for pilgrimage, but, more importantly, to treat people suffering from cholera. That disease generally broke out at the mela and always found Bhai Nathu Singh at Hardwar, administering his famous black pills to those afflicted by it. He cured thousands.

Stories of his success spread far and wide. And in course of time, these reached the Whitehall in London also. The secretary of state, who used to rule India from over there, advised the viceroy to convey the appreciation of his majesty's government to Bhai Nathu Singh for the yeoman service he had been rendering to humanity. And so, one day, a letter came to Bhai Nathu Singh. It was marked 'On His Majesty's Service.' Bhai Nathu Singh was frightened. He thought that some summons had come to him from the *kacheri* (court) on the complaint of someone on whom his pills had produced some adverse effect. But when the meaning of the letter was explained to him, Bhai Nathu Singh jumped with joy.

God knows who suggested it to him, but soon thereafter we saw a big placard hanging on the wall behind him inside his small shop. It carried that letter and below it announced in bold letters in Urdu and English, 'Bhai Nathu Singh's famous black pills for cure of cholera. Recognized by His Majesty's Government in England.' Bhai Nathu Singh never charged any money from anyone. Senior to me in age by decades, he must have by now become a dear departed soul. And he must have carried with him the secret of the ingredients that went into the making of his pills.

IN LIFE AND DEATH

KRISHAN KALRA

PANDIT BISHAMBAR LAL was the official Pujari in the Sanatan Dharam mandir at Sargodha, a small town in West Pakistan. Bishambar Lal was not only the Pujari; he also doubled as the *Shastri* and read from the scriptures every afternoon. He wasn't there because he had bribed any high-powered managing committee or because his father before him had done the same job. He was there simply because the people of Sargodha loved and admired this humble man, who was their friend, philosopher and guide in many difficult situations.

Panditji as he was fondly called by everyone in the town had been the Pujari for five decades. He took care of the *moorties* in the *sanctum sanctorum*, while his wife the Panditayan swept and scrubbed the rest of the modest temple. He was there when the people visited the temple early in the morning; applying tilak on their foreheads and giving out *charnamrut* and *prasad*.

Later, he would make house calls for various pujas, *shradhs*, betrothals, marriages, *mundans*, births, deaths wherever he was needed. Afternoons were reserved for discourses from the scriptures; first reading *shlokas* in Sanskrit and then translating them in simple everyday Punjabi. Evenings again, people came to do obeisance especially on Tuesdays and Panditji would be there to help them. He was indeed a part of life of everyone in the sleepy little town. And for all his pains, Panditji got only two simple meals a day and a few sets of rough homewashed kurta-dhoties. The man just didn't want anything else for himself. All collections in the *mandir* went to charity.

One morning, while doing his *surya-namaskar*, after the routine daily bath at the canal, Pandjitji collapsed and died instantaneously. Other bathers rushed to help but there was no life left in the old man. The saintly man had departed peacefully without any fuss and without any botheration to anyone; so typical of his life. Someone ran and got a *tonga* to carry the body to the *mandir* and the one-room apartment behind it where the old couple lived. Another person informed the lady.

As the body was kept in the *mandir* courtyard, Panditayan came and quietly touched her dead husband's feet. In a low composed voice she told the gathering to wait for her as she also wanted to 'accompany her husband' to the cremation ground. "Give me a few minutes to get ready," she said and went into her room. People were aghast. Women did not go with funeral processions those days. Yet, she had asked them to wait, so they didn't have a choice. Half an hour passed but there was no sign of the old lady. All arrangements had been made and they didn't want to delay the cremation. They would again try to dissuade her once she came out.

One of the ladies went and knocked at the door. There was no response. She knocked again, still there was no response. She pushed the door gently; it was open. Inside, the Panditayan sat in *samadhi*. As she touched her shoulder the lifeless figure just rolled onto the floor. The woman shrieked and more people rushed inside. Someone felt for the pulse. There was none. The lady had indeed succeeded in "accompanying her husband" on his final journey.

EARLY BIRDS

MOHINDER SINGH

WE HAD A RULE. We'd reach a Delhi dinner party 'punctually,' i.e., precisely 30 minutes after the given time. Quite often we found ourselves the first to arrive. "Are we too early?" we'd mumble. To which a genial host would respond soothingly, "Someone has to be the first." And, after getting a nod from his mate, would start dispensing drinks. Once we surprised a hostess busy feeding her dog.

In the light of such experiences, coupled with an elevation in bureaucratic rank, we have now taken to reaching an hour late. (Amazingly, we can't help fret and fidget over every minute of our guests' delay beyond the invited time.) And yet we find ourselves among the first few.

Often the 'important' people arrive even later. Perhaps it merits some research as to how there's always a minimum gap of 30 minutes between the arrival of the 'powerless' and the entry of the 'powerful' at a Delhi dinner party. If the 'powerless' somehow start delaying their arrival, the 'powerful' automatically adjust their timings too.

Does this time synchronization flow from a sixth sense? Or is there a miraculous method by which the information gets relayed? About punctuality at dinners, Germans probably represent the other extreme. Posted as consul-general in Hamburg, whenever we asked a few couples to dinner at 7.30, the doorbell would ring at 7.30 sharp. As one opened the door, all the invited couples would troop in. Not a coincidence, we learnt. Guests arrive a few minutes in advance and wait in their cars; they don't want the host to be distracted by opening the door separately for each invitee. And they would send their gift of flowers during the daytime, so that the hostess could use these instead of buying them.

Arriving punctually at a Delhi dinner party has another feature to contend with. You have at the minimum two solid hours of liquid refreshments. And here operates a general rule: The more plentiful the liquids, the more deferred the solids. Incidentally, alcohol is an item at dinner on which a host and hostess may be putting conflicting interpretation. The more he succeeds in dispensing alcohol, the more he expects jollity. Yet a very 'jolly' guest is rarely in a position to appreciate a quality meal. A bit dismaying to a hostess who had stood an hour before the butcher's counter selecting choice cuts and laboured hard to plan and organize an elaborate meal.

SPELL AND TELL

SHEELA JAYWANT

THE COMPUTER MAY have made my editing assignments speedier, but detailed proofreading is a must to avoid howlers like "eating facts and oils are not good for the health." Some go into press inadvertently and no one notices, for they seem to mean something. Sub-devotional magistrates, streaming hot noodles, breathlicking sights, and 'heat' of the matter, are amongst those.

At other times, the word or phrase seems to make sense, but one pauses over it nevertheless. Like the story of a deer that was 'last in the woods,' of abuses that were exchanged in the 'heart of the moment,' of vital military plans that were 'shaved' for political reasons, or someone who left 'early in the mourning.'

Is the computer intelligent enough to test us semi-literate humans? Is it actually playing games or trying to teach me something new? I came across 'pair-pressure' in an article I had written on arranged marriages. I had used 'peer'. But when I read what the screen flashed, I found it actually made sense in that context. Another time, feeding in material on air safety, the computer invented 'helicopter rotters'.

Going through a manuscript on expeditions in the Himalayas, there was an incident written about where the climbers found two abandoned tents. Whilst playing about with the words, the computer chose 'where (we) met up with two tents'. Considering that the tents did save some lives, it seemed fair to give them a personality.

Sometimes, an error is not corrected because the computer can't find anything wrong with the meaning or the spelling. That's why in one article about the Dalai Lama, who, when discussing the fate of his people, also contemplated other 'masters' (measures) for their welfare.

The world's 'widest' police was how the Goan police was described in one story. The next read-through revealed that it was the world's 'wildest' police. The sentence had to be deleted, for I had lost track of what the original was. Describing a person who was very anxious, my PC declared he was 'raped' in worries. Elsewhere, it said a pregnant lady's abdomen was 'frightful', swollen. The same woman's husband, being the only male in the queue at the gynaec's, stood in splendid 'insulation'. In the same article, I read about a sterile 'goes' and about a blanket wrapped at the 'west'. The computer found nothing wrong with either.

Sometimes, what the computer says is truer than the real things. For instance, whilst trekking in jungles, it informs me, there's nothing as exciting as coming across a herd of deer, or a solitary wildcat or beer (bear, actually, but the bottled stuff could be just as fun). Equally true, in an article on agriculture, was the story about 'irritated' fields of rice. Or the one on diarrhoea, which spoke about 'lost' stools. Perhaps the computer is actually smarter than I am. That's why I depend upon it for a livelihood, for my spell cheques.

ONE DROP OF INK

RUSTOM VAZIFDAR

SHANKAR*JI* HAS BEEN in our family longer than I. The family I was born into. From the days when he drove our soft-top Austin, then Morris Minor, Fiat and now Esteem, he has been more than just our driver. Our cars are always clean and rarely require anything more than the regular services. I do believe no one in my family knows when the cars were last serviced and when they are due next. That's Shankar*ji's* job.

It has never been a problem for our entire family to go on a holiday together. Shankar*ji* is always there to look after our house, our dog and our fish tank. He knows all our relatives and friends, and all our relatives and friends know him. He can be relied upon for all our errands, whether it is picking up a child from school or depositing money in banks, or delivering some important document to our clients. Or for that matter the daily shopping for my wife, who never bothers to ask an account from him, because she knows he has never cheated us and never will.

So I was rather surprised one day when my mother said, "Pity, if only Shankar had not allowed that one drop of ink to fall." She is the only one in the family who calls him without the '*ji*' suffix. I was intrigued and asked her what she meant. "Well," she replied, "if you put one drop of water in a bowl of ink, it will make no difference. But if you put one drop of ink into a bowl of water, the entire water will be blemished forever." "What has that got to do with Shankar*ji*?" I asked. And she told me this story.

Many years ago when Shankar*ji* was a lad of 17, he got involved with a gang which made counterfeit one-rupee coins. This must have been in an age when one rupee was considered a princely sum. The long hand of law caught up with this youngster who had gone astray, and he was jailed for two years. After his release, Shankar*ji* could not find anybody who would employ him because of his criminal past. His father, who was working as a sweeper in a shop near our office, one day came to my father, pleading his son's case, swearing to be responsible for his behaviour. Whether it was pity or just good judgment of character, I do not know, but my father employed Shankar*ji* as an odd job boy.

Years passed, and he was taught driving, more out of necessity than to better his future. And as our family grew, Shankar*ji* played a significant part in bringing up my two sisters, me and our children. I remember as a lad, getting a clip across my ear from him when a particularly foul word escaped my mouth. Today long after my father is no more, Shankar*ji's* character is as clean as a bowl of water — except for that one drop of ink, which he will have to take with him to his grave.

RAW PITCHERS

VN KAKAR

"HAVE YOU LEFT your child-producing machine also back in Peshawar?" my grandmother would ask me almost every other day. In the morning when my wife would go up to her to seek her blessings, she would survey her with great expectations, caress her head and whisper, "May your husband remain eternally alive and worthy of his youth, and may you have seven sons!"

Later, while my wife shared household work with my mother, she would reprimand my mother for not doing anything in the matter. "Why don't you show her to some hakim? More than a year has gone by and there is no sign of any baby coming. In this much time, I had one in my lap and another on the way."

One morning, my wife was overcome with nausea. My grandmother jumped from the bed, dashed towards the bathroom and sprang like a doll. Thereafter, it was my wife and my wife alone who became the centre of grandma's attention. "Don't do this and don't do that," she would say and drum a hundred and one things into her ears. Crushed almonds were mixed in the milk that was forced on her morning and evening. The parathas served to her were made in pure ghee despite the fact that we just couldn't afford that. We had started life afresh almost from scratch. Partition was only a little behind us.

Hamidullah and his wife were a charming couple in Lucknow, famous for giving lavish parties. At one such party my wife whispered to me that something was happening to her and we must go back home at once. I took her in a cycle-rickshaw, and back home my father and father-in-law — the former a retired army officer and the latter a serving one — took charge of the whole operation and handled it on war footing. A lady doctor was called from the military hospital and our first unborn baby terminated its journey towards life somewhere midway.

"Take it easy, young man," said the lady doctor to me, as she came out of the room in which she did to my wife whatever was needed to be done. From that point onwards, grandma took my wife almost in complete custody. Days, weeks, months passed. Whenever I showed some inclination of getting a bit close to my wife, grandma would rush to her aid and tell me bluntly, "Never, never commit the blunder of pouring water into a raw earthen pitcher."

Almost 50 years have gone by since then. It could never occur to me then that my last assignment in the government of India, as the media adviser to the ministry of health and family welfare, would be to help prevent the birth of babies in the entire country. Loop, condom, pill, sterilization, abstinence, rhythm, *brahmacharya*, coitus interruptus — what is it that I have not preached? But could anything match that 'raw earthen pitcher' advice that my grandma gave to me long before family planning was officially launched in the country?

LETTER FROM SANTA

NARAYANI GANESH

IT WAS CHRISTMAS eve. I shut my eyes as I sank gratefully into the bed that was the venue of a vicious pillow fight only an hour ago. The last of my guests had left after dinner, taking their raucous children with them.

"Amma, have you put the stocking out?" my six-year-old daughter inquired anxiously, as she tiptoed into my bedroom. No, I hadn't — I'd forgotten all about it. "Of course I have Sonali. Go to bed," I said. I could see her skipping back to her room. I dragged myself out of bed, my mind a blank. What was I to do now?

It all started when a nursery school-going Sonali confronted me with the question: "How come I never get any presents from Santa Claus?"

"We never hang out stockings so how could poor Santa know that there was a child in there, waiting for presents," I explained. So we fished out a huge sock and pinned it to the front door. Once she was asleep and we filled it with toffees and crayons. This was repeated the next year, only, the presents were different.

I rummaged through the cupboards but found nothing that could interest a six-year-old. Then I got an idea. When we were shopping the previous week we'd seen a 'singing' book for Rs150 — it had a mock keyboard that played nursery rhymes. I'd thought I'd get it for her later. I sat down and wrote a letter from Santa: "Dear Sonali you've been a good child. So I'm going to make your wish come true. Here's Rs.150, to buy that musical book you saw at the store last week with your mother. Love, Santa". I rolled the letter with the money stuffed into the stocking, hung it on the door and went back to sleep.

Sonali was delighted with Santa's letter. We went out and got that book which she showed off to her friends for months afterwards. The following Christmas I planned ahead; we even got a Christmas tree — a tradition we still continue with.

"So are you happy with Santa's gifts this year?" I asked her. Rolling her eyes she said: *"Nee daane Santa?"* (Aren't you Santa?) She knew it when I got that letter from 'Santa' last year.. but please don't stop playing Santa, Amma..." Giving me a quick hug, she ran off to play with her friends. I smiled sheepishly at Maya, my older daughter and co-conspirator, who couldn't stop laughing....

AMITABH BACHCHAN

SHASTRI RAMACHANDARAN

HE WAS NOT the 'Big B' then. He didn't even want the B-word to be written after his A-name. He wasn't a superstar. He just had stars in his eyes.

Mrinal Sen had finished shooting *Bhuvan Shome* (1969) in Bhavnagar. He was editing the film in Bombay and went over to friend KA Abbas' house. Abbas had just started work on *Saath Hindustani* and was sitting amidst a group of the proposed crew and cast. Sen tells him that he is looking for a voice for the narrator of his film. He could have gone to the Films Division but would rather try a new voice.

A lanky young man moves out of the seated group, comes up and says *"Ami Bangla jaaney"* (I can speak Bengali). Sen tells 'the boy' his Bengali is bad but his voice is good and that the narration is to be in Hindi. Abbas allows him to do the job. Job done, Sen says he will pay him, but not much.

The boy is not keen on the money and protests against payment. Sen insists and pays. The boy wants to know if his name will appear in the credit titles. Sen says, yes. Boy says his name is Amitabh Bachchan. "But put only Amitabh. Leave out the Bachchan." Sen agrees.

In the credit titles of Mrinal Sen's *Bhuvan Shome*, voice-over artiste 'Amitabh' appeared at the very end. Perhaps, the only film in which Amitabh Bachchan's name figures last and not even in full. The famous baritone voice of the narrator is heard for a total of about three or four minutes, at the beginning and the end. Seeing Sen's film in 1970, I didn't notice this 'detail'. And wouldn't have paid any attention to it 30 years later had not Mrinalda told me the story. At Delhi's India International Centre, where nine of his 26 films, including *Bhuvan Shome*, were shown; thanks to 'Thethe' Lalsawmliani Tochhawng, of the IIC Film Club which has been recently recognized as the best film society in the northern region. The retrospective of Sen's films in the Capital — the last one was in the 1980s — was also an occasion to catch up with Amitabh Bachchan's past.

Bhuvan Shome went on to win many awards, including the National Award in 1970. That year, when the two met in Calcutta, Sen asked Amitabh to accompany him to a felicitation at the Bengal Film Journalists' Association. Seeing Amitabh, a reporter asked whether 'he' was his 'next hero.' Sen replied, "I like him very much. I have to find a character that fits him".

Amitabh himself was keen on acting in one of Sen's films. He would have liked a role in *Interview*, and Sen would have liked to cast him. "But I wanted an ordinary-looking person. And Amitabh, even then, was an imposing personality."

Does 'the boy' remember all this? Of course, says Sen with fond recollection. Bachchan recently corrected a journalist that the first voice-over he did was not in 1983 for Satyajit Ray's *Shatranj ke Khiladi* but for *Bhuvan Shome*. "But Amitabh said I paid him Rs500. He does not remember. It was only Rs300." The 'Big B' no longer needs to keep track of a hundred or two.

GOAN TALK

SHEELA JAYWANT

A PILOT IN Goa is one who owns or rides a motorcycle taxi, that unique local mode of transport. Until a friend revealed what the word meant here, I used to wonder why neighbours gave my husband curious looks when I said he was a pilot.

As recent arrivals in this lovely little western state, we were amused to read familiar Hindu names spelt unusually. 'Purxottama' and 'Xembhu' were easy to decipher, but we needed help to read 'Quenim' as Keni. It took a couple of months to get used to names like Conceptao de Souza a Quadros Ferrao. And to know that 'Joao' was pronounced zoo.

The first time a shopkeeper asked me whether I'd like a rupyacho Gandhi, I was foxed. He owed me a buck and didn't have change. I was willing to accept a toffee worth the amount. But a Gandhi worth one rupee? Curious, I said yes, and received a small, white postal stamp with the brown profile of the Father of the Nation on it.

'Rupyacho Gandhi' accurately describes the value of the man in the country today. Once, trying to cajole a colleague, I said, *"Koi Baat Nahin."* He kept quiet for a moment, then wondered aloud why I'd chosen that moment to confess that I hadn't bathed. The same colleague was puzzled when I described someone very fair as *gori-chitti*. *Gori* he knew was fair, but *chitti* meant letter, hence the confusion. Films have popularized the Hindi language, but since many here have not learnt its grammar and vocabulary, there is often misinterpretation of the words. For instance, the innocent phrase *Kamaal Hai* slipped out of my mouth one day. At that, the acquaintance I was conversing with appeared visibly shaken. Why, she demanded, had I called her "*Kamaal Hai.*" It took many minutes before we sorted matters out. She had heard and seen people use these two words in Hindi films. The voice that spoke them was always raised and so were the hands of the speaker. She had assumed they were abusive swear words.

In an identical situation, another friend thought I was being nasty when I said to her, "*Hudd Ho Gayee.*" She thought *Hudd* meant a female canine. Again, the reason for such an assumption was lost in a Bollywood movie she had seen sometime, someplace, whose language she had not quite followed.

What is more interesting though, is the evolution of phrases that are not found even in neighbouring Maharashtra or Karnataka, which are only a couple of minutes' drive away. One such is the quaint greeting that all Catholics extend to the Hindus during the Ganapati festival. "Happy Ganesh," they say.

It is like saying "Happy Christ" at Christmas, I pointed out to a friend, for it doesn't make sense. Perhaps not to outsiders, she said. But couldn't I just gracefully accept the warmth behind the greeting? Why dissect and analyse the hows, buts and whys of it all? Ah well, I had to agree with her and now when anyone wishes me "Happy Ganesh", I reply with a nasal, musical "Thankuaahn", just as anyone else would.

BORIS'S 300

JUG SURAIYA

LONG BEFORE THREE-TON Sehwag was a distant gleam in the BCCI's eye, there was another exclusive group which called itself the '300 Club' in what was still Calcutta. This was when the sun still shone on the Raj, of which Calcutta was the second city after London. If London was, as Dr Johnson once called it, the most 'clubbable city' in the world, Calcutta came a close second.

Of the many clubs Calcutta spawned, perhaps the most legendary was 'The 300'. It was the brainchild of a White Russian adventurer called Boris Lissanevitch, who at various times had been a fighter pilot, a trapeze artist, a chef, and a ballet dancer with Diaghilev's troupe. In Calcutta in 1967, Boris tried to get me to loan him Rs2 lakh to start a pig farm in Nepal. "Pigs. That's the future," urged Boris, in vain. Rs2 lakh was an unimaginable sum for me, futuristic pigs notwithstanding.

Boris got together a consortium of Maharajas who helped found the '300 Club', which in terms of exclusivity, threw the gauntlet at the feet of London's celebrated '400 Club', which was so called because membership was restricted to that number. By implication, Boris's 300 was even more selective in its rights of admission. As narrated in Boris's biography, *Tiger for Breakfast,* some half dozen founder members of the 300 undertook an 'anthropological' expedition to Hollywood to conduct a field study of the subspecies known as the 'starlet', with particular emphasis on their vital statistics. The expedition was a great success, to the satisfaction of all concerned.

Housed in a turreted mansion on what was then Theatre Road, the 300 became famous for its all-night parties, which culminated in a breakfast of bacon and eggs, said to be the best in the city. Sometimes, there were literally gatecrashers. As, for example, when a high-spirited Raja smashed his sports car into the gates of the club and tottered into the bar demanding a double peg, ek bloody dum. Boris's friendly pet python, slithering about the premises, is said to have caused many a late-night reveller to take an oath of abstinence or otherwise.

The real serpent in Eden, however, turned out to be World War II and the flood of allied servicemen it brought in its wake. The 300 hospitably opened its door to many of them, only to be left with a heap of unpaid bar bills as evidence that its assets had literally been liquidated. Where silken gowns had once rustled, all that was left was a *dhobi's* clothesline straddling the unkempt, deserted grounds; the flapping laundry a ragtag flag flying at half-mast for departed glory. Boris went on to set up the Royal, Kathmandu's first hotel. But that, as they say, is another story for another club evening.

AT LOVE'S GATE

GK SHARMA

JAGADHRI GATE IS to Ambala City what the Gateway of India is to Mumbai. Fortune-seekers from foreign lands or sailors from neighbourhood disembarked at the Gateway of India, to be welcomed to the fabled land of the Orient — Inde or Hindustan. Jagadhri Gate, too, was one such welcome arch in the Purbia heart of undivided Punjab — now Haryana. J Gate greeted in its portals Indians from all corners of India and even foreigners who came to invade our land.

A lot of history or popular tale is attached to J Gate. The spot became famous because this was the place where invading armies of Ahmed Shah Abdali pitched their tents before their final onslaught in the battle of Panipat. Mango groves or plantations nearby made it known as '*Amba wala*' — a heralder of the sprawling city of Ambala.

When Abdali's forces won and were marching back to their homeland with looted booty, they camped again here. Abdali thought of bequeathing a structure of "victory arch" as a gesture of gratitude since final preparations had taken place here. Also, the *jagirdars* of Jagadhri (a nearby town) had helped Abdali militarily and monetarily. Hence, the arch was named "*Bab* (gate) Jagadhri."

Down the ages J Gate has welcomed millions as the first national highway (GT Road), built by Sher Shah Suri from Calcutta to Peshawar, took a bend right opposite it. At present, it is only a halting stop for buses.

But J Gate is more famous for a romantic tale. This is a true story. It happened 40 years ago. A young man in his twenties was madly in love with Paro. Both had taken vows never to separate. The boy was happy that his parents had persuaded the girl's side for marriage. But the uncle (*maman*) of the girl didn't approve. He was scheming and secretly managed to marry her off to another person. Information reached the boy somehow.

He dashed to J Gate from where the bus had taken his screaming Paro to another destination, probably never to return. The boy was too late. And in a state of shock he would search and run after every departing bus till he would get exhausted. For months and years, the boy was seen doing the same, love-lorn, his hair overgrown and flowing down to the waist. He started parting his hair in the middle into two braids just like his beloved, decorated them with rainbow colour ribbons — obliterating the difference in looks (physically)!

Years have turned him into a Sufi bard, singing his clarion call (in Punjabi) : "*Oh, Sohnien, hun tan main tera roop dharan kar liyaie... wapas aaa jaa J Gate.*" (Oh my beloved, I have changed myself into your lookalike... now come back to J Gate.)

History does not bother me. Abdali or Suri — both must take backseats. I know and recognise J Gate as a monument of incessant, unremitting love. The lover boy is now an old man in his '60s — his hair has gone grey and dishevelled, hanging aimlessly long. But his zeal for meeting Paro has not diminished a bit. Four decades have gone by, but he is even today seen limping slowly after every departing bus, still hoping his beloved Paro would come back to Jagadhri Gate.

NAMES AND NUMBERS

SUKANYA SINHA

OUR TRIPS BACK to India during the Christmas vacation always seemed too short and hectic. We would be hopping from one relative's house to another, staying barely long enough to exchange greetings and make unsuccessful attempts to refuse the four *rosogollas* inevitably offered at every home. This time we were headed for our last stop for the day, my husband's aunt's house in Shibpur, a suburb of Calcutta.

His aunt had recently moved to a new house and we had not been there before, but we were armed with the new address — 10, Katapukur Lane. It sounded simple enough. We got off at the Shibpur bus-stop and finally located Katapukur Lane and proceeded to look up the numbers on the houses.

This proved to be more complicated than we thought because number 9 was followed by 9/1/1A and next to it a 9/3B was tucked around the corner. We were stumped, but walked on, confident that in spite of the bizarre numbering, we were getting closer to 10. But after number 9/3B came 11. It looked like house number 10 simply did not exist. We were perplexed and at the same time a bit offended. This non-existence of number 10 seemed an affront to our sense of order and symmetry. An elderly gentleman with greying hair sat reading a newspaper on the patio of number 11.

"Excuse me, we are looking for number 10. Could you show us where it is?" I asked. He looked up from his newspaper with a puzzled expression on his face as if the question made no sense to him.

"Whom do you want to meet?" he responded.

"Well, we are looking for number 10 Katapukur Lane. Your house is 11, the one before that 9/3B. What happened to number 10?" I asked again.

Ignoring my question, he asked us once more whom we had come to meet. Giving up hope of solving the mystery of the missing number, I told him that we were looking for Mrs Meera Banerjee. His face lit up with instant recognition.

"You mean the lady who works at the bank and has a daughter who is getting married next month?"

"That's the one!," we concurred.

"Why didn't you say so in the first place? They live in that red house right around the corner," he said.

We thanked him and walked up to the red house and rang the bell. As aunty opened the door I glanced at the number plate. It was number 10 indeed! The old generation's reaction reminded me that there is more to a Calcutta address than a street name and a number. The existence of a house here is defined and shaped by the people who live in it. How could I have forgotten my old neighbourhood where the houses on our side of the street had the address of Motilal Nehru Road, and those across the street were labelled Manoharpukur Road and nobody found it odd? We knew who lived in every house and that was all that mattered. At the same time, I remembered the neat sequential row of numbers on the mailbox in my apartment building in New Jersey. I knew all the numbers of the apartments around mine, but though I tried hard, I could not remember the faces and names that went with them.

BIBLIO MANIAC

DILIP RAOTE

SOME OF MY strong prejudices surfaced recently when I was getting a valuable document photocopied. The 19th hole — to use golf terminology — who operated the machine picked up the document as if he were about to make a cone to hold roasted *chana.*

"Hey! Be careful," I shouted. The slob gave me a dismissive look, and flashed a welcoming smile at the next sucker who'd just walked into the shop. Having copied one side of the document, the operator turned it over with as much diligence as a butcher slamming a slab of meat. I wondered what the man's punishment would be in afterlife.

The Greeks and Romans of Alexandria surely meted out summary punishment to sloppy copiers. The Alexandria library had half a million scroll-books, most of them copied like our college kids photocopy imported textbooks. Alexandria had its version of Xerox centres, and ships entering port had to submit any books on board for quickie replication. The librarians and ship captains couldn't have taken kindly to scribes who returned mutilated originals. Perhaps they were crucified, a most popular curative treatment in those days.

After years of observation I have classified mutilators, especially of books, into turners, spitters, doggies, marginalists and underwriters. Since I spend a considerable time amid books, I encounter these horrors far too often and they do nasty things to my BP. It's because of them that I ceased to lend books. Turners are the so-and-so-'s who can't bear to look at both pages of a book together. They fold the book on the binding so they can hold it in one hand and have only one page in front of their nose. Spitters are like bank tellers; they need to wet their fingers to flip paper and the tongue is the nearest wet surface available. Doggies have poor memories. They can't remember the page at which they left off, nor do they possess bookmarks. They fold a page corner to mark the interruption and give books the dog-eared look. Marginalists are failed academics. They annotate books with profound thoughts in the margin such as 'why?', 'Check this', 'Says who,' 'Imp,' or worse. The most unforgivable lot are the underwriters. Like poor readers who move lips and trace words with a finger, underwriters read with the help of a ballpen. Every phrase, sentence or para that stimulates them must be underlined. They drive me crazy.

Instead of the text, it's the underlined portions that hold my attention. After a few pages of this torture I give up and return the book to the library. I feel sorry for libraries. I suppose it's impossible to revive crucifixion in these days of Amnesty and human rights watch. But we need something comparable. Perhaps the mutilators could be sentenced to being recycled into paper for books. That would be atonement. Nah, it's too good a fate for them. I think they should be recycled into toilet paper, nothing less. I told you I have strong prejudices.

FEELING UNLOCKED

SUNIL GUPTA

APART FROM THE friendly neighbourhood burglar, it is the museum curator who knows most about locks and keys. In the seven years since I've held custody of precious art I've handled locks of all moods and strengths. Of course, along the way one has had to suffer a lot of torn pockets carrying sharp-angled keys.

On a normal day I set out to work in the museum armed with a two-and-a-half-inch brass master key which prises open a heavy seven-lever lock on the door of the painting reserve room which serves as my office. Once inside, there are more locks to confront hanging upon cabinets and almirahs. Of various shapes and sizes, these fasteners have been assorted over the years, and quite a few of them are old and exotic enough to qualify as museum displays in their own right. So, when a number of old locks were phased out recently I did not send them to be sold for scrap.

The curator's instinct urged me to hold the quaint locks for posterity. I have a collection of 20 in a plastic bag in my cupboard. I often take the mechanisms out to oil their innards. Spread out on the working table, the antiquated locks seem like so many small denizens of a mettalic world. There is one that completely detaches from its U-shaped hinge. Another has the appearance of an iron sling ball smoothed and darkened by many hands. A few of the contraptions, especially those with little sliding metal strips covering the keyhold, bring back memories of my ancestral home in a north Indian village. I am reminded of thick wooden doors and iron shackles and locks with shuttered keyholes hanging below the crossbeams.

There are deep mysteries in the way the old locks worked. My gallery staff would set about opening showcases with an attitude bordering on reverence. It was never taken for granted that the locks would release their grip at the first turn of the key. If such an augury did come about, the happy event was always attributed to the 'generosity' of the lock. And when the levers refused to move the cause was yet again vested in the 'stubbornness' of the fastener. Apparently, this irrational conception is not uncommon in professional spheres.

Recently, I read about a motorcycle racing champion who selects his bikes on 'mood' and 'feel,' rather than specific performance parameters. I could, of course, brush aside such sensibilities as deriving from superstitious mindsets. I could call my attendants a gullible lot. The old locks are nothing but defunct contraptions and this explains their behaviour.

The point, however, is different. I am drawn to the belief my attendants have in their 'illogical' perception. Really, I wonder, is the metaphysics of a situation more relevant than its practical processes? I am now more inclined to think so. And this new-found faith of mine goes right down the line, to the old and retired utilities on my table. Yes, the least I can do for these exhausted warriors who've silently guarded my paintings is to deny their oblivion in a scrapyard.

QUILT WARMTH

NITI PAUL MEHTA

IN WINTER IT is good to have a shawl around you. A blanket is even better but there is nothing to beat the luxury of the humble *razai* if you want to stay really warm and cosy through the long chilly winter nights. It can embrace you from all sides and can provide you warmth from head to toe.

In the villages of Haryana and UP you find people with their *razais* wrapped round them even while attending to their daily chores, looking much like small mobile huts or like the snail who carries his home with him.

Over the years there has been a perceptible change in the attitude of the people. Modern-day youth find the traditional *razai* clumsy and cumbersome. They prefer a sleek and thinner version of it. A guest who had to spend a chilly December night under such a quilt shivered even as he narrated how he survived that night.

"I thought I'd freeze," he said. "So I slipped under the mattress. The *razai* and the mattress together saved me." Of late, however, the quilt seems to be back in favour. Even the trendy ones who thought it below their dignity to carry a *lehaf* with them are virtually wearing it as a fashion piece. The utility of the humble quilt seems to have got the better of its clumsiness. Many a youth of both the sexes can often be seen wearing stylishly quilted jackets and even gowns. An international company is now marketing 'intimately quilted warmers'. Indeed they promise that the inner wear produced by them is 'as warm as love'. A *razai* ought to be attractive and inviting, something it'd be pleasant to slip under. So often the cloth used in making a *razai* has bright colourful, flowery patterns on it. Padded with soft cotton, down or feathers, it is stitched with delicately contoured cross lines of stitches, making exquisite designs and patterns to enhance its overall beauty.

The quilt cannot speak, but if it could, it would tell some of the most fascinating tales of love and romance. Ismat Chugtai, the controversial Urdu short-story writer, has immortalized this humble winter bed-piece in her story, Lehaf, depicting a lesbian relationship between a nawab's wife and her maid.

In places like Aligarh, people have a way of measuring the intensity of cold. When the mercury dips a bit but not too much and the cold is of moderate intensity, somebody might be heard saying, "*Ek fard ki sardi hai.*" (It is cold but a single shawl is enough to bear it.) As the temperature dips further, the measure, too, registers a corresponding rise. Thus it can be *do fard ki sardi, teen fard ki sardi* and so on. Under severe cold conditions, experienced in the first 10 days of December last, it can even become *paanch fard ki sardi* (enough cold to justify being wrapped in five shawls). But there is no such thing about a quilt. One is enough — for one or both.

ABIDE WITH ME

RK PARASHAR

TOMBS HAVE ALWAYS fascinated me, especially of great men and women and of those by whose side they were laid to rest. Shah Jahan, for example, is said to have wanted to build for himself a mausoleum of black marble on the opposite bank of the Jamuna at Agra, facing and matching the white Taj Mahal he had built for his beloved queen, Mumtaz Mahal. On his death, he was instead made to share space for his grave with his queen in her mausoleum in the awe-inspiring, candle-lit, incense-filled crypt deep in the earth. As I stood there I felt like an intruder who had trespassed the privacy of a royal chamber.

The tomb of Aurangzeb, the last great Mughal emperor, was an entirely different experience. As per his wishes, he was laid to rest by the side of the grave of his spiritual mentor in an ordinary grave, open to sky, on which grass grew. This even though his chief queen's sprawling mausoleum, known as *Bibi ka Makbra*, was situated not far away. An aura of dignity in death and an ambience of tranquillity and peace pervaded the place making one feel a kinship with the buried. The tomb is located in a madrasa in Aurangabad.

The most bizarre tomb that I have come across was in the district town of Burdwan in West Bengal. The story goes that Prince Salim the future Jahangir was so enamoured and infatuated by the beauty and charms of Mehr-un-nisa, wife of Sher Afghan, a Pathan nobleman, that after ascending the throne, on the pretext of insubordination by Sher Afghan, he sent an army under the command of Qutb-ud-din, the governor of Bengal, to chastize the former. In an affray that took place, Qutb-ud-din was killed and Sher Afghan hacked to pieces by Qutb-ud-din's soldiers. In a case of rather black humour, the two antagonists were buried side by side. I am inclined to believe that if there are ghosts, it is not unlikely that every night the ghosts of Sher Afghan and Qutb-ud-din rise from their graves, engage each other in combat and on the break of dawn re-enter their respective abodes to tend to their wounds and curse their fate for their company in death. As for Mehr-un-nisa, Jahangir married her in due course, made her his chief queen and bestowed on her the grand title of Noor Jahan the light of the universe.

The two most unique cenotaphs that I have seen are on the grounds of the Aga Khan Palace in Pune. During the Quit India Movement in 1942, Mahatma Gandhi was kept under house arrest in this palace. With him were his wife, Kasturba, and his personal secretary, Mahadev Desai. Desai died there after a short stay. After a while, Kasturba also fell ill and passed away.

In order to avoid any political fallout of their deaths in custody, both were cremated in the palace premises itself. Two small, ordinary-looking, pillar-like cenotaphs were constructed in their memory. It is touching to behold these two cenotaphs, erected by the Father of the Nation himself in the memory of two unrelated persons very dear to his heart.

BRIDE-PRICE

VIDYA VENCATESAN

MY GREAT-GREAT-great grandparents were married rather young. The deal was struck at their respective parents' wedding. Fortunately for both parties concerned, my ancestor Appavayyar arrived ten days before his bonny bride, Mangalanayaki. The engagement was soon conducted and a princely sum of rupee one exchanged to confirm the betrothal. When the bride and groom turned five, the day following his thread ceremony, Appudu as the little man was fondly called and Manga as she called herself were pronounced man and wife.

Of the three-day festivities, the feisty Manga remembered only two things: a silk *kunjalam* (an equivalent of modern day fancy ribbons that keep plaited tresses from opening out) and gold *jimikais*, both gifts from her mother-in-law. A heavy *taali* or *mangalsutra* was tied round her neck with solemn instructions never to remove it.

As was the custom, the child bride stayed on at her parental home on the other side of the Kaveri till she came of age, while her child groom was given visitation rights. For every festival that featured on *thealmanch*, the little man came right over, astride on his doting mother-in-law's hip. The Hindu scriptures regard the son-in-law as the eleventh incarnation of Lord Vishnu and the child groom reveled in the role. Everybody bent backwards to please this little son-in-law, his wish was their command. But all this was not enough for him. His heart was set on his bride's *kunjalam* and *jimikais*. Oh yes, long hair and pierced ear lobes are not an invention of the MTV generation as they so fondly imagine. No sooner did these words leave his lips than the little woman was stripped of her meager bride-price. She resisted valiantly, shed copious tears but they would hear nothing of it.

He was her Lord and Master, they reminded her. The true implications of marriage sunk in at last. Enough was enough, she decided. When they went out to play that evening, she chased him through the woods to the river bank trying to yank the *kunjalam* off his hair. She proceeded to threaten him to an early watery grave if he ever so much as looked at her priced possessions again. The terrorised little husband swore to do, as he said, till death did them part. Alas, that his better half could not swim either, he did not find out till very much later.

Spring melted into summer and the years rolled on. His child-bride matured into a beautiful woman. She cooked his meals, bore him children, kept house for him; but a docile obedient wife she was never to be. They disagreed on everything and their fights were legendary. After 85 years of blissful strife or strife-filled conjugal bliss, a dozen children and an impressive number of grandchildren and great grandchildren, Appavayyar's beloved Manga left him to meet her Maker. Family lore has it that the old boy lost heart. He ate little, slept even less for the next ten days till life ebbed out of him. I do not believe in life after death, but on stormy nights when thunder rolls and lightning crackles, I imagine the two must be at it again.

CORPORATE CUES

RITA PINTO

THREE YEARS AGO, the chairman of Home and Hearth Inc. offered me the post of executive director of the company. The offer was made in very convivial surroundings, but my acceptance was ensured by the firm pressure of his fingers in my arm. The duration of the employment had no retirement age. The job was guaranteed till "death does me part." This exalted position did not merit discussions on remuneration in monetary terms. I was, however, assured that all my expenses would be met unquestioningly.

With adjacent living quarters, I would be on 24-hour call. It was subtly pointed out that not all corporate executives are lucky to have a bed provided on office premises itself. How much I have availed of that facility may call for another 'middle'. As with all up and coming business conglomerates, the gestation period would be about ten years before I began to enjoy the "fruits of my labour".

The company only guaranteed job satisfaction. Job responsibilities matched terms of employment. I would be solely responsible for the growth and development of the two staff members in a manner that would enable them to replace me as I approached senility. I was only cautioned about the trade union leader. The only one capable of bringing the company to a grinding halt, she required to be dealt with an iron fist in gloves. The personnel package thus defined, my foray into corporate politics began. Three balance sheets later, I have put an end to lightning strikes by the union leader. Verbal warfares by the two staff members are now replaced by treaties, and the chairman's "I take the bouquets, you catch the brickbats" attitude is now doing a volte face.

Liaising with the various governmental organisations — the ration office, postal department, MTNL, MSEB, and of course the educational institutions where the staff were being sent for training, has sharpened my killer instincts to a degree where the chairman prefers operating out of the company's premises.

Home and Hearth Inc. has not only prospered in this declining economy but is now poised for take off. The staff are more than ready to declare me senile. The union leader is determined to undermine my position, she being convinced that my handling of industrial relations would see the death of all trade unions. The chairman, honing on my performance and potential, is increasingly distancing himself from the company.

Three appraisals later, the chairman in consultation with the staff, has rated my performance 'excellent'. Given a choice, they would not replace me with all the Bill Gates' of the world. And I have received the final accolade, a green-signal to print my own visiting cards. The designation to be printed would be of my choice: 'managing director' or 'housewife'.

UPS AND DOWNS

ANUPA LAL

I LEANED BACK in the jeep with a sigh of contentment. It had been a good four days, away from the filth and clamour of Delhi and I had savoured the balmy mountain air, the cheerfulness and hospitality of the ashram. Shri Bhuvneshwari Mahila Ashram, founded in the '70s as a refuge for destitute women and children, now runs a health and education programme in four districts of Garhwal. I had accompanied an old friend who visits the ashram every month as an adviser, and was most impressed by the good work being done.

Is it easier to be good and do good in a salubrious climate and sylvan surroundings, I wondered idly as we drove down to Rishikesh. Suddenly the jeep slowed, and we saw four bodies being pulled out of the Ganga. A truck had rolled into the river the night before. Another few kms, and the jeep came to a halt to join a long line of vehicles. There was a major landslide ahead, which people said might take two days to clear.

Now, we could forget about taking the train from Dehra Dun to Delhi that evening; or drive back to the ashram and wait there till the road was motorable again. Or we could send the jeep back, take our courage — and our belongings — in both hands and cross the landslide. With Satish and me, was Aditi from the ashram — young, energetic, unafraid. She took my small but heavy suitcase, and we joined those scrambling up and across the landslide, even as a few more rocks came hurtling down.

"Hurry!" said a man behind me. I had lost Satish and Aditi in the crowd. "I'm trying," I said, "Just take this please." I thrust at him one of the two bulky plastic bags I had. To my surprise, he carried it without murmur, along with his own things. A strange sense of unreality had by then enveloped me. It wasn't city spoilt, sedentary me, scrabbling for hand and footholds in shifting rocks, but a frozen-faced stranger with a thudding heart.

Not once did I look sideways and down at the swiftly flowing holy of holies, so terrifyingly accessible from where I was. Finally, the ordeal was over. Filthy, shaky, but alive, we resumed our journey, packed like sardines into a strange contraption, posing as a taxi, which got us to Dehra Dun well in time to catch our train. Once comfortably ensconced in the Shatabdi, clean and civilized again, I thought of Aditi, who, unasked, had carried my suitcase along with her backpack across the landslide. I thought of the stranger into whose hand I had unceremoniously thrust my overloaded plastic bag. I thought of those who, like Cyril, the ebullient, enigmatic secretary of the ashram, have chosen to work, away from the bright lights, to make life brighter for those less privileged. And I felt rather small. Then I thought of all those at either side of the landslide who had just stood there watching. And I felt better. I might have covered myself more with mud than glory, but I had got myself across!

TABLA THERAPY

ANIL EKBOTE

HAVING COMPLETED HIS internship and becoming a full-fledged doctor, Ravi Kumar joined his father, Dr Ram Prasad, and began to practice at their clinic at Mallepalli in Hyderabad. One evening, some men carried in a patient. The man was well-built, but had suffered a stroke and was able to walk with great difficulty and much help. Though Dr Ravi Kumar had seen patients in worse condition, he felt particularly sorry for this one. For, this patient was the renowned tabla *nawaz*, Ustad Shaik Dawood, who had accompanied three generations of musicians, including Fayyaz Khan, Bade Ghulam Ali, Roshanara Begum, DV Paluskar, Bhimsen Joshi, Savai Gandharva and Ravi Shankar. Besides, he was also a close friend of Dr Ravi's father, himself a singer and an acknowledged connoisseur of music.

As Dr Ravi examined him, the Ustad in his slurred speech casually asked "*Sangeet mein koyi dilchaspi hai*?" ("Do you have any interest in music?") The doctor nodded and told him that he had learnt a bit of tabla. To the Ustad's pleasant surprise the doctor had had his lessons from one of his own *shagirds*. "When I get well, I myself will teach you tabla," the Ustad declared.

Dr Ravi gave a polite smile. Later, he advised the patient a regular round of physiotherapy. "You can even play the tabla," he suggested, "It will be good for your fingers and wrists." The Ustad's escorts helped him out of the clinic. Several days passed. One Sunday afternoon, Dr Ravi suddenly found Ustad Shaik

Dawood, now looking much better, standing at the gate of his house. The Ustad had caught him playing cricket with a group of children of all ages. Handing the bat to a child and wiping the sweat off his neck and face, Dr Ravi murmured apologies and took the Ustad in.

"I have come to teach you tabla," the Ustad straight away announced. Dr Ravi was stunned. Certainly, while at his clinic, the Ustad had told him that he himself would teach him tabla. But Dr Ravi hadn't taken the Ustad's words seriously. He had never imagined that one day the Ustad would suddenly arrive and make good his promise. This was an opportunity which could not be missed at any cost. As Ravi took in all this, the Ustad, as usual clad unassumingly in a kurta-pyjama, smiled and added, "The walk here and a lesson in tabla will be my physical therapy. You've advised it, haven't you?"

There was a flutter of activity. The tabla was taken down from the shelves and dusted and tuned. A few beetle-leaves were brought. Ustad Shaik Dawood took a length of red thread from his pocket and tied it on Dr Ravi's wrist. To complete the traditional ritual of the *ganda*, Dr Ravi offered his new guru a token amount of money and with that he became Ustad Sheikh Dawood's *shagird*. And with that the Ustad began his regular physiotherapy.

MUM'S THE WORD

A MADHAVAN

SOME PEOPLE ARE unforgettable characters for me, not because I admire them particularly but because I always remember the books I have lost to them.

At one stage of my life, I and my wife were lodged in a ministry hostel in New Delhi, cramped into a room, with much of the luggage stacked on the balcony. I jealously guarded a few paperbacks and some hardcovers from my student days which I hoped to study for my edification in future.

We came to know a younger couple living nearby. We enjoyed their company, and with them liked to raid the Bengali Market for a treat, going Dutch, or amble through the Purana Qila.

It was not long before they called on us in our small, transit residence. While my wife was making tea, the visiting lady drifted to my shelf of books by the balcony. She examined some of the books and exclaimed, "Oh, you've got this. May I borrow it?" It was a volume of short stories by Somerset Maugham.

During the week that followed, whenever we met I tried to guide the conversation gently to literature and fiction, so that I could casually ask, "By the way, how did you like the Maugham?" This led to hilarious evasions on her part and frustrations for me. Once while walking around when we were caught in a shower, I referred to the famous Maugham story Rain, but the lady smartly blocked my gambit by humming the theme song of the film *Barsaat*, immortalized by the young Lata. Another time when we were sitting in a cafe at tea-time, I brought up the title of the novella *Cakes and Ale*, only to be deflected into a pointless discussion on the difference between ale and beer and draught beer. Always the chatter turned to the foibles and follies of the people we knew or to politics, cookery and fashions. I felt I was constantly falling off the razor's edge.

One day my wife and I paid a return visit to our friends. They lived in a small flat. It did not take me long to sidle up to the almirah in the corner, where some art objects were displayed, such as a Japanese doll and a crystal bowl from Prague, along with a row of books. My eyes quickly registered a set of three uniform Penguins. Yes, they were volumes two to four of the *Collected Short Stories of Somerset Maugham*. And yes, volume two was unmistakably mine. The lady glided across to me, breezy as ever. "Oh, you are looking at my books? You know, I am making up a set of Maugham stories. Only volume one is missing."

We valued her friendship too much to say a word. Years later, I succeeded in buying a copy of the lost Maugham at a flea market in Bonn, and thus completed again my own set.

GENE JUNCTION

TANUSHREE PODDER

I WAS BROWSING through the greeting cards at the shop when I noticed her. It was her confident gait and her funky hair-do that caught my attention first. I blushed with embarrassment when she caught me staring at her, and walked away to the opposite end of the shop but I couldn't resist glancing furtively at the perky teenager. Her angelic face somehow seemed familiar. And then I noticed the tight pair of jeans she was wearing. I was stumped; it was unbelievable. There it was, leaping out at me from the back pocket of the girl's jeans, the bright embroidery I remembered so well. It was the pattern of a colourful Chinese dragon breathing out flames. My brain did a double take. Could there be another one like that?

Although the bright colours of the threads had faded over the years, I knew it was the same. The funky teenager was wearing the pair of jeans I had owned about 18 years back. I saw my initials intricately embroidered on the dragon's tongue. They had been made to look like a motif of oriental origin by the expertize of the Chinese tailor whose nimble fingers had worked on it. I had bought the jeans at a small shop on the Serangoon Street at Singapore. Those were the days when the designer labels had not hit the shops in our country and we, youngsters then, were starved for a pair of good jeans. The only ones worth boasting about, came from the counters selling imported stuff. The first thing I had done on my trip to Singapore was to buy a decent pair of jeans with the limited foreign currency I carried. I recollect the sense of pride I had felt as I tried them on. I will never know what had inspired me to get the motif embroidered and stitched on the back pocket. Maybe it was the brush with the mysterious oriental air and an overdose of bestsellers that made me request the shopkeeper to get a dragon embroidered and patched on the jeans.

Those days not many people flaunted such patches, and back home I became a celebrity of sorts. I swaggered down the road, showing off the designer patch on my pair of slim-fit jeans. It never failed to attract envious glances. It was my best friend who had finally managed to steal it from me. For her wedding present, she had specifically demanded my precious pair of jeans. Although it tore my heart to do so, I had to part with my prized possession because I loved her dearly.

I lost touch with my friend after my father got posted out of the city. She had also moved on in life. And now, as I followed the teenager out of the shop, I knew why I had found the face so familiar. It was the face of my dear friend and I was happy to have traced her, at last — through her daughter who was wearing my jeans.

TELL-TALE WEDDING

SUREKHA MOHAN

ARRANGED MARRIAGES HAVE held their ground in this country and among the Indian diaspora abroad despite the steady onslaught of western values and culture. The matrimonial ads that flood our dailies prove that unlike in the West, marriage here is seen as too serious an institution to be influenced by purely passion.

Recently, my brother came home from the US, tied the knot and flew back with his bride. It was an arranged match. The alliance was given the green signal by the family elders before the two youngsters took over and got acquainted over the phone and through e-mail. Of course, they could have put their foot down if the match was not up to their expectations. This was not so in the past when in most cases, youngsters had no choice but to comply with the wishes of the family elders. In fact, instances were not uncommon where the bride and the groom had their first glimpse of each other in the marriage *pandal*.

In this context, there is an interesting anecdote related to my uncle's marriage. The year was 1959. My uncle, who was working as a senior teacher in a district high school, received a proposal from a girl of a well-cultured family. She was also a teacher. Everything seemed just right and the alliance was cleared. But then some tongues started wagging. People, who had seen the girl, wondered how a fair, handsome and personable young fellow could marry "such a dark-complexioned, average-looking" girl.

These comments put uncle in a dilemma. He had not 'seen' the girl nor did he have the guts to make such a proposition. At the same time, he did not want "to be saddled with an ugly duckling". It was at this juncture that my father, his younger brother and confidant, then a college fresher on vacation at home, volunteered to help. For the adventurous, brash, strapping youth, this seemed just the right chance to have some fun and brighten up an otherwise drab vacation.

He went on the sly to the school where the lady worked, posing as a student seeking admission. With the help of a fake letter of recommendation from a common friend, he met the lady, spoke to her and even secured admission in the school. This was not surprising considering that in those days, admission formalities were not so elaborate and complex as it is now. To make a long story short, much to the bewilderment of the family elders, uncle dilly-dallied until he received father's nod.

After that when the marriage was solemnized, father, who was not one to shy away from anything, suddenly developed cold feet. He still vividly recalls the beat his heart skipped when he was 'introduced' to his sister-in-law. In the lottery of life, though aunt proved to be uncle's jackpot, he never thanked father. To do so would have violated the pact of silence that brothers feel bound to uphold. Nevertheless in the sign language of family, father knew and they moved on.

GENERAL KNOWLEDGE

JUG SURAIYA

IT WAS IN the 1970s. I was a reporter for JS magazine, and my editor, Desmond Doig, sent me to Nagaland. It was a challenging assignment. Insurgency was at its height. As I travelled through the state, I encountered a surreal world of fugitive rumour and shadowy propaganda. I interviewed Nagas from various walks of life, from local MLAs and village headmen to self-professed militants of the underground. They all agreed on one thing: If the Union government wanted to win the hearts and minds of the Naga people, why had so many Army personnel been posted there so as to make it seem like occupied territory?

Indeed, camouflage green was everywhere, merging into the lush vegetation of the landscape; convoys of trucks, troop carriers, heavily armed jeep patrols. Estimates varied as to the actual numbers. Some said there were 30,000 troops in the state, others multiplied this by five. In the absence of hard fact, I tried the Army authorities in Kohima but without luck. "Confidential information," I was curtly told.

So I came back to Calcutta, and wrote my report. The then general in charge was outraged. He called me into his office and read me the riot act. How dare I publish unsubstantiated rumour as fact? Was I an anti-national, a subversive element? I assured him I wasn't, and offered to do a follow-up report to set the record straight if he'd provide the relevant facts and figures. Divulge sensitive information, compromise security? Was I mad, unpatriotic, or both? was the horrified response. I tendered humble apology and bowed myself backwards from his office.

A couple of weeks later I was invited to dinner at Desmond's. Among the guests was the General, who fixed me with a gimlet eye and enquired after my seditious tendencies. As the evening progressed, however, he got into a mellower mood and gave me some avuncular advice about curbing one's curiosity. Knowledge is power, and power is responsibility, he said. I nodded in acquiescence. By the end of the evening the General had warmed to me to the extent of offering to drop me home before returning to his residence. As we got to his car, the General told me that he and his driver were totally unfamiliar with Calcutta's streets, barring major thoroughfares, and asked me to direct his chauffeur. Which I did, taking a tortuous route of tangled lanes. We got to my place, I hopped out, thanked the General for the ride.

"Oy, how the devil do we get back to the main road from here?" came a cry from the car.

"Why, just go back the same way we came," I replied.

"But we don't know the way we came. You've got to tell us!" expostulated the General in his labyrinth.

"Knowledge is power, and power is responsibility", I intoned.

"Bloody hell!"spluttered the stalwart soldier, envisaging a night of wandering the streets in forlorn search of home. Magnanimity towards a routed adversary is a civilized norm. I gave them simple directions to the main road, barely 50 metres away. Since then, the General and I have bumped into each other more than once and exchanged cordial greetings. Both of us respect the other's right to know. Should need arise.

CRISIS GAME

K SUBRAHMANYAM

I WAS DEPUTY secretary (budget & planning) in the ministry of defence in 1965. At that time I was offered a fellowship in strategic studies in the department of international relations in the London School of Economics (LSE). The government permitted me to accept it. I was all set to go and had just signed the sale document for my car at about 10am on Monday, September 6, 1965 when my RAX rang. I was informed that early that morning the Indian Army had launched its counter-attack in Lahore sector. I immediately sent a note to the defence secretary offering to cancel my LSE assignment. After much hesitation over two weeks he accepted my offer to stay back. The LSE was good enough to renew the offer in the following year, and I was in LSE in 1966-67.

At that time politico-strategic gaming was very fashionable in the strategic community. I was one of the dissenters from the popular view about the utility of such gaming. My view was that strategic decisions are culture-bound. Therefore, Americans or British playing games about how Indian and Pakistani leaders would react to various crises could not be anticipated correctly by them.

It so happened that one day I spotted a book *Crisis Game* by Sidney Giffin displayed for sale on the pavement outside the LSE. I picked it up and found that it dealt with two crises — one in Cuba and the other in Kashmir in 1966. I sent the book to the government of India. They could not obtain a second copy since the publishing house, Doubleday, said they had sold out. In the

'Crisis Game' played in early March 1965 in the Institute of Defence Analysis in Washington DC with the participation of the Harvard University, India loses the war. Prime Minister Lal Bahadur Shastri was portrayed as a weak and indecisive leader. After defeat, India is compelled to accept a UN plebiscite and mediation by the United States. I felt vindicated that the game as well as the actual events that followed proved my thesis. The only copy of that book is today kept locked safely in the Institute for Defence Studies and Analyses, New Delhi.

The 1965 Pakistani plan to launch the war was within the knowledge of the US government and they did not warn India. In fact, they had played a military game and concluded that US Patton tanks would smash through the Indian armour. When the Pakistani Pattons were destroyed by the obsolete Indian Centurions and outdated Shermans, the Americans were livid. I recall the then head of the US military supply mission in Delhi, Maj-Gen Johnson, himself an armour man, denouncing the stupidity of the Pakistani divisional commander who rushed headlong into the Indian tank trap at Asal Uttar. That was in response to my upbraiding the US, the self-proclaimed arsenal of democracies supplying weapons to Pakistan to be used against the world's largest democracy. That was on September 14, my brother's birthday. On that day, he was one of the fighter controllers at Halwara Air Force station, which was being bombed two to three times a day by US-made aircraft with US-made bombs.

GOOD-FOR-YOU GUINNESS

NOEL LOBO

"ASSERT YOURSELF. DON'T let them bully you and don't stand for any nonsense from anyone." She meant well and followed up with advice on my body language sending the wrong signals; and my reluctance (inability?) to tell people off when they are impertinent.

Pondering these pearls delivered on the day that Alec Guinness left for another shore, I thought of his three delightful books of memoirs totally ignored in his obituaries. Read them if you get a chance. In the last of them, *A Positively Final Appearance*, he tells of his looking forward, on reaching three score and ten years, to, well, to avoid tedious repetition, acting on the advice directed at me in the opening salvo of this piece. Alas, he found he just couldn't. Me too; I cannot. Having reached the age of 70, I find it impossible to round on one who patently deserves it. Would a man with any pretensions to officer-like qualities say to a subordinate, as I used to, "Consider yourself bottled." (Bottle: slang for a naval blast.)

In his first book, *Blessings in Disguise*, I find something else that I unwittingly shared with him. As an actor in the 1930s, desperately looking for work, he used to tramp the streets of London, his shoes in his hand to save the soles. Years later as an RIN cadet in London on leave on a pound a day I saved not on shoe leather but on the tube fare from our genteel club, the Bernhard Baron Officers' Club, to Leicester Square where Lyon's Corner House offered spartan fare for my supper. I used to walk there; and having got there helped myself — it was a self-service cafe — to the cheapest dish on offer. Supper in two bob. Now I am not making this up: The great actor was also in the navy. For the duration of World War II, whereas I was in it for life. And the positively final link — in a manner of speaking —with Sir Alec was the forest rest house half way down the hill from Kandy to Colombo where I spent a night in 1958. This is where he too had stayed while part of the film which brought him cinematic fame was shot a couple of years earlier.

A farewell to Sir Alec with a delightful story of him, as a lieutenant, RN, bringing his landing craft to secure to a wooden stump in a muddy creek in Malta as ordered. Repeated attempts to throw a rope having failed, he bawls at three shadowy figures barely discernible in the dark on shore. "Don't just stand there. One of you take the rope and put it round that post." No response whatsoever. "Frightened to muddy your boots, eh?"

At this taunt, one of them stepped forward and did as ordered. "Thank you," this came sarcastically from Lt Guinness. To his horror he catches a glimpse of red tabs and medal ribbons galore. It was Field Marshal Lord Gort, the governor of Malta.

STRIKING ABBREVIATIONS

ZAFAR IQBAL

ABBREVIATIONS WERE INVENTED as an aid to memory. In earlier times it was just the educational degrees that you wore on your gowns that mattered: BA, BSc, MA, MSc, PhD, LLB, etc. Then came the twice-born service, the Indian Civil Service, the ICS. And what a most coveted three-letter word it became. For reasons best known to the heavens, 52 years ago, the 'Civil' component was replaced by the 'Administrative' element to create the IAS. This, too, did acquire a great halo. The Indian Police Service was born before the Indian Postal Service; so you have the IPS vs the IPoS. But, the Indian Forest Service and the Indian Foreign Service both have to fight it out for the IFS.

The government departments and their working brought forth many an abbreviation. There used to be the draft of a ministerial note, then the second draft and then the final draft. Hence the shortening of the words. You had the public works department become the PWD, but which soon acquired the more notorious renaming as 'public wastes department'. You have the MHA, the ministry of home affairs, which has the misery of running home affairs. The PM rules through the PMO, and this office handles more mail than the GPO.

The DMs and the DCs acquired a credo of 'Don't Mingle' with the public and then 'Don't Care' for them, too. CEOs have now become the COOs. VIPs have become VVIPS, and ZVIPS.

Then came the Americans. You have the USA, US, NASA,

NATO, etc. We also have the UNO, UNICEF, UNIPOM, UNCTAD, WHO and what not. The FBI simply became the Feds. The CIA is more dreaded and active than the KGB; and successful, too, for it was the KGB that had to be unlettered. A laudable World Wildlife Fund has been reduced to World Wrestling Federation.

Our own RAW is no match for the ISI. Even though the Indian Standards Institution has been rechristened the Bureau of Indian Standards, most people want the ISI-approved make. In Bombay more people will take the IAS for the Indo-American Society and the ICS for the Indian Cancer Society. Time was when people were scared of IT raids, and now the same people are chasing IT. And we must all help CRY. The film world cannot be left behind, and we have the memorable HAHK, DDLJ, DTPH, KKHH, PBDHH and now KNPH. But nowadays we cannot tell whether AC/DC refers to currents or people.

RECYCLING WASTE

VINOD TAKSAL

"AND WHAT IS that, Mr Deshpande?"asked the new Resident Commissioner, peering under the staircase at an iron contraption in a blanket of cobwebs.

"A cycle, Sir," responded Deshpande, the Establishment Officer.

"Clear that out. I don't want junk lying around here", said the RC.

"Where shall we put it, Sir?"

"Put? I am asking you to throw it out, dispose it of..."

"But it's government property, Sir. To dispose it of, I need sanction..."

The RC's glare made the EO tremble. "No, Sir, I mean sorry Sir, but I need sanction from Mantralaya..." The RC clearly didn't like being told of limits on his powers.

"Get it then," he said. Next day, a letter went out to Mantralaya: "Whereas a cycle was purchased for official work only...and whereas the cycle had remained unused and unusable since peon Ganpat's retirement a decade ago...kindly sanction may be granted to dispose of the said piece of government property." Three months later, Mantralaya replied pointing out that under rule – , section –, subsection – "sanction cannot be granted to sell/dispose of any government property without prior authority of the AG's office." Out went a letter to the AG's office, which in turn sent a proforma to be filled in triplicate "prior to sanction for the disposal of, by way of sale or any other manner of any government property." This complied with, the EO waited for the sanction. But the AG's next communication, after several reminders, didn't contain the sanction. Instead, AG wanted the original receipt for the cycle and a copy of the sanction for purchase. The EO was livid. Two years had passed, the precious sanction hadn't come and the RC was relentless in his taunts. Over the next week, curtailed to three days owing to the CM's one-day 'working visit', the EO turned his office upside down. But the receipt and the original sanction could not be traced.

Crestfallen, he informed Mantralaya. Months passed. The rusted frame was by now haunting the EO. The end-of-tenure transfer put an end to his nightmare.

Some months later, the Mantralaya sent a stinker. The loss of the receipt and the purchase sanction was a grave dereliction of duty, it said and asked the EO to "show cause as to why action should not be taken against you". The recipient of this was Deshpande's successor. Collecting his wits, the new EO wrote back that: he was not the EO who had sought to dispose of the cycle; the receipt was not with the *Sadan* as under the rules the original with the purchase sanction had to be deposited with the AG; and the responsibility for loss of the two documents must, therefore, rest squarely with Mantralaya.

Nothing was ever heard from Mantralaya. Then one day, a new RC was heard telling the *safai karamchari:* "*Yeh cycle yahan se uthake le jao.*" A few months later, the RC asked the Finance Secretary, accompanying the CM on a day's working visit, "Ranga, please sign this. It's about that stupid cycle." The note solemnly stated that "the said piece of government property is untraceable, and, therefore, the file is closed."

OUT OF LINE

NANDITA DOGRA

IN THE GOOD old days before soccer hooliganism replaced it, queuing up was the national pastime of the British. Personally, I too am a champion of rules and order provided I am the one who has laid them down. The Brits have since relaxed though not sufficiently, as we shall see later, but the pro-discipline lobby need not lose heart.

Queuing up is alive and thriving, thanks to the Japanese. In fact, it is to the credit of people from the land of the rising sun that despite (or, is it because of?) their punishing schedule to attain unparalleled economic miracles, they have found the time to perfect the low-brow art of queuing up.

During a trip across Europe I too witnessed the uncrowned shoguns' mastery of queues. Most tour coaches have an annoying habit of reaching the same service station at the same time. During these brief halts on the highway for petrol, foodstuff etc., there would invariably be a rush towards the sale counters but only by the non-Japanese. Even at the risk of missing the coach departure our young fellow-travellers from Japan would not deny themselves the joy of patiently standing in an orderly line, bemused at our unruliness. Be it currency exchange, sandwiches, chocolates, souvenirs of 'Le Shuttle' or Swiss bells, the queue was sacred; even if there were only two persons facing a counter long enough to accommodate several burly, disgustingly ebullient Americans. Indians, on the other hand, know better than to live life in such an orderly manner. Why line up neatly when you can rub shoulders and soak up the warmth of fellow beings? We do not do so intentionally. Far from it. We are a peace-loving nation and we value social order more than anyone, and often anything, else.

Queues are symbolic of discipline and being crazy about symbols we are all for it. It is just that our worldview of personal space is somewhat different. When asked to queue up we do it quite enthusiastically except that the line we form contains not one column but many. (When asked not to, we do it with greater zeal as in flights long before the landing time.)

Typically two to three persons stand next to one another or in a zigzag manner chatting, muttering under their breath or just sizing up the person ahead of them. Rising on tiptoes (and frequently on other's toes) every few seconds to monitor the speed of the counter staff also comes naturally to us. Given our innate 'tolerance' we find nothing strange about it, but this 'fellow feeling' is not appreciated in the West. Once at Heathrow airport the help desk staff got so exasperated with me and two other Indians that the specific order to form a 'single file' was followed by a 'live demonstration'. Methinks it was much ado about nothing but in true 'Indian' spirit I have forgiven them. And I can now queue up in both Indian and Western (read Japanese) styles.

JAGGERNUT TALES

KISHORE BHIMANI

I HAVE SEEN Mick Jagger three times since my college days — he was enrolled for a BSc (Econ) at the London School of Economics. Quite predictably he did not complete the course. He was there for a mere six months before hitting 'golden disc' fame with *It's All Over Now.* He perhaps felt the same way about the LSE. Recently he referred to the old school as the "temple of the Toffs". But back to my run-ins.

The first was at a Test match between England and the West Indies at the Golden Isle of Barbados in the 1970s. (The Rolling Stone loves cricket and chases a good match to the ends of the planet Earth.) In fact our Mick is an earthy sort, never averse to a bit of chit-chat and obliging with his autograph, unless one of the ladies is around — Gerry Hall, for instance, or Bianca. But, while I wanted to ask him about the Rhythm n' Blues revival, he would only talk about Boycott's tedious batting.

The second was at Lord's in 1988 when his drummer, close friend and fellow sinner, Charlie Watt, insisted on leaving his leader in Paul Getty's box and travelling with me to the media area from which Watt was promptly thrown out. The two of us, then, spent the pre-lunch session in the Denis Compton Stand alongside the old-timer who was busy putting out wagers on Kempton Park races during the day.

The last was in Calcutta, three years ago when he arrived at the city's watershed disco incognito with a string of beefy 'minders', the kind that would have made Laloo Prasad Yadav's personal security look like choirboys. I managed to get a quick "Hi and bye" and elicited a pasted-on smile from him in the sweaty environment. My companions for the evening were perhaps a bit disappointed. But after all, what did they expect? Mick to discuss old times like Professor Valentine's boring lectures or the Malthusian theory as interpreted by Professor Sir Lionel Robbins? Or perhaps, and herein lay the rub, his unauthorised and highly controversial biography by arch-critic Christopher Andersen? I sometimes wonder what would happen if Mick and Chris met up somewhere lonely.

Talking of controversial things, since they are going to question 'everyone' in the match-fixing imbroglio, they might as well query the Rolling Stone. Apart from gathering no moss, he might even tell them about what he heard "under the Boardwalk." His credibility might be more acceptable than that of Chris Lewis and the Indian event manager who talked to the English bowler of yesteryear.

LAXMAN'S REKHA

VRINDA NARAYANAN

DEAR MR LAXMAN,

First of all, let me apologize for not having taken your permission to let Imagination follow Mr Common Man. I have always wanted to know how Mr Common Man managed to be just an expressionless onlooker at the goings-on around him. In fact, I have always been intrigued by Mr Common Man and therefore couldn't, but help let Imagination follow him. The task was made very easy as Mr Man had thought himself to be too common.

The day started early for Imagination. Mr Man, as usual, around 6am, set out for his morning walk. He headed for the neighbourhood park where he saw Mr President, of the Resident Welfare Association (RWA), talking earnestly to the park *chowkidar*. Mr President seemed to be persuading the *chowkidar* to part with a few seedlings, kept in one corner of the park and which were in all probability meant for the beautification of the park.

Incidentally, Mr Man had purchased the same seedlings, just the previous day, from the RWA's nursery, being maintained in another corner of the same park. Oblivious of the fact that he was being watched, Mr President handed over a few notes to the *chowkidar*, and had said, "Let this be for your *naasta paani.*" The *chowkidar* had then simply handed over the seedlings, seedlings over which he was to have kept a watch. Imagination noticed that Mr Common Man had been expressionless. Around 11am, Mr Man went to his neighbour, Mr Raman's house. Mr Raman belonged to the defence services. The telephone linesman was restoring life into the telephone, which had been dead for a month. When the work was done, Mr Raman shoved a bottle of whisky into the outstretched palms of the linesman and said, "For your *naasta paani.*" Mr Common Man continued to remain expressionless.

Around 2pm, Mr Man was in his car, waiting for the signal to turn green. The traffic policeman was questioning an old man of about 55 who looked very familiar. Mr Man soon recognized him to be Mr Minister, and by the look of things the policeman too seemed to have recognized him. Mr Minister simply removed a few notes from his pocket and slipped them into the policeman's hand. He added, "Let this be for your *naasta paani.*"

The law-enforcer had let off the lawmaker for breaking the law. Mr Common Man continued to be expressionless. Around 7pm, Mr Man was at the local temple. Standing next to him was Mr DDA with a leather bag in hand. Mr Man was wonderstruck at his presence in the temple of a person rated as the world's most corrupt. Mr Priest, the executive secretary to God, had overtly shoved a huge wad of notes into his leather bag saying, "Let this be for your *naasta paani.*"

God's residence was undergoing some renovation and expansion. Mr Common Man's face was swept by a range of expressions in quick succession. Mr Laxman, I sincerely hope that this is only a figment of Imagination's imagination.

ONE IN A MILLION

KRISHAN KALRA

SOME FRIENDS CALLED the other day to congratulate us on our wedding anniversary. A few days later it was my birthday. So, once again, there was a round of calls. At times, we've even had parties to celebrate such special occasions — a 100-odd guests, booze, good food, gifts and much merry-making. Of course, we are not the only ones to do so; indeed everyone celebrates such occasions. Landmarks like silver and golden jubilees and 60th or 75th birthdays become even more special; justifying bigger dos.

The futility and insignificance of all this, however, hit me the other day while working on some demographic data for a study.

Suddenly I realized that there is really nothing 'special' about such days. The world population is around five billion. On a rough estimate, 70 per cent should be married — give or take a few hundred million. If we are to assume that an equal number of marriages are solemnized every day of the year —notwithstanding the Hindu penchant for auspicious days — that works out to nearly five million wedding anniversaries every single day, day after day. So, next time you send out invitations for your wedding anniversary, do bear in mind that some of your guests may have a million or two other invitations also.

Birthdays are even more crowded. Whereas you need to have a wedding anniversary — and that too after you are a major — birthdays are a lot simpler, solo and no age bar either. Making the same assumption once again, on each of the 365 days in a year there should be about 14 million birthdays. And I am not even counting dogs and other pets whose birthdays are also celebrated in style. No wonder, greeting card companies do roaring business. Of course, they offer cards for other occasions too — Valentine's day, Mother's day, Father's day, Teachers' day, Xmas, New Year, Diwali, Gurpurab, Eid....you name it. And the latest I hear about are 'JLT' — Just like That cards.

Hindu mythology tells us about 8.4 million life forms on this earth — humans being just one of these; and, how the soul goes through all these before being reborn as a human, the supreme form which is capable of thinking and doing something for others. Of course, for saints, there are short cuts like *mukti* — being the ultimate release from this painfully long cycle of 8.4 million births and deaths. But, even in *mukti*, one is just a star in the sky, amongst millions of others.

Talking of stars and moons, planets and galaxies, distances in millions of light years, meteors and black holes, imagine the whole incredible celestial panorama. How small and insignificant — not even one in a million — does one feel in the midst of all this gigantic, bewildering, mind-boggling, ultra-complex set-up which seems to be working on its own.

THE BRAHMARISHI

KS AMBI

IN THE TOAST proposed by President Clinton at the dinner to Prime Minister Vajpayee he referred to India as a global player and to an alliance between India and the US which will change the world. Till recently the US always hyphenated India-Pakistan while referring to this region. In the 1960s India was written off in the book *Famine-1975* and there was an expectation that it would break up.

After the 1971 war and Pokhran I test India was referred to as a regional player. In recent years, India has been repeatedly told that its nuclear weapon status would not be recognised. Against this background the Clinton toast comes as a surprise. It brings to mind the story of King Vishwamitra who finally became a *Brahmarishi* (brahminical sage of the highest order).

India is named Bharat after Bharata, the son of Shakuntala, Vishwamitra's daughter. King Vishwamitra, a Kshatriya coveted Kamadhenu, the cow which gave limitless food and was, in the possession of Vasishta, the Brahmarishi.

His attempt to physically seize Kamadhenu was frustrated by the spiritual might of Vasishta which could not be matched by the armed might of Vishwamitra. He, therefore, decided to give up his kingdom and become a *Brahmarishi.* Up to that time only brahmins became *Brahmarishis.* He was determined to achieve that status through penance. That was not easy. He became first a *Rasjarishi* (kingly sage) and then a *Maharishi* (a great sage). He was determined to become a *Brahmarishi* and to be addressed so by no less a person than Vasishta, the authentic *Brahmarishi*. He underwent numerous trials and tribulations which prevented him from accumulating the power of *tapasya* to the extent required to become a *Brahmarishi*. First, he was tempted by the heavenly *apsara*, Menaka. He succumbed and thus was Shakuntala born. That reduced the power of his *tapasya*. Then he promised to send King Trishanku in his mortal body to heaven. But when Trishanku was thrown out Vishwamitra stopped him from crashing down to earth. Instead, he used the power of his *tapasya* to create an intermediate *swarga*. That was the second setback. Finally, he achieved the status of *Brahmarishi*, became the preceptor of Rama and got him married to Sita. Vasishta accepted him as a *Brahmarishi*.

One wonders whether Bharat had been doing penance all these years to achieve the status of *Brahmarishi* — a global player — and to be addressed so by the most powerful *Brahmarishi*, the United States. Our *tapasya* consisted of pluralistic democracy, economic liberalisation, high growth trajectory, nuclear and missile capabilities and IT prowess. Sceptics may question whether one should take at face value the various friendly pronouncements of the present president of the US.

But even if the US establishment has perfected the art of ambiguous pronouncements, in an open society and established democracy it is not easy to play such games over a period of time. Now that Vasishta has accepted this Vishwamitra as a *Brahmarishi*, is the latter in a position to perform that role? Or does Bharat have to perform more *tapasya*?

GANDHIANA IN ITALY

C UDAY BHASKAR

CASTIGLIONCELLO, TUCKED AWAY on the Tuscany coast in the northwest of Italy, was the least likely place for me to visit but it was venue for a conference on 'New Challenges in the Spread of Weapons of Mass Destruction'. Paolo, our affable host, steered us through a lavish dinner where the wine flowed freely. As the only vegetarian, I was an oddity but the lady serving me was more than solicitous.

The contrast between the idyllic surroundings of Castiglioncello and the destructive nature of the subject under discussion was striking. Predictably, the India-Pakistan nuclear tests of 1998 and Kargil topped the agenda. Later that evening, sitting on a large rock on the Mediterranean Shore, chewing my cigar, I reflected over the arid session. From the Pakistani perspective, India was the only challenge and castigated as the original sinner. Would this bitterness ever change?

The vignette of daringly (un)dressed bathers with not a care frolicking on an affluent Italian beach-front seemed incongruous with my muddled thoughts about the Indian subcontinent. From a distance a couple greeted me, "Senor Indiano." Had we met? Yes, she was the young lady who helped me at dinner and we re-arranged ourselves on the rock. Julietta and her fiance were on holiday. She had just finished art history while Francisco was teaching in a Pisa school. Neither of them had visited India but were keen about it and soaking up. Francisco's grandfather was apparently influenced by Gandhi and had become vegetarian. I told them about the seminar —WMD seemed such an arcane acronym in the setting we were in. Julietta, the more curious, said she had two queries. One was about Gandhi, the apostle of peace, and the bomb. Would he have approved of India's actions? I replied tentatively.

Gandhi abhorred the bomb and championed disarmament but was also against all forms of discrimination. He would have expected India to raise its voice, even if it meant standing alone in urging the major powers to renounce their exclusivity and climb down the nuclear ladder. I speculated further. As a pacifist, he would not have cheered the bomb but as a supreme realist, Gandhi may not have disapproved of India's conversion to deterrence, since it was embedded in the philosophy of disarmament. Deterrence was a means, perhaps less than honourable, but inevitable if India wished to retain its autonomy, assuage its WMD insecurity and pursue ultimate disarmament. We are committed to principles, I exulted, as Francisco translated, though to be honest I wondered how Gandhi would have responded to the current reality.

The second query, she persisted. Sure thing, any question, fire away. Is it true, asked Julietta that India is one of the most corrupt places in the world? So says a recent report, but can a country that produced Gandhi and is so committed to principle — as you said — be so corrupt? I winced as she turned the blade further. Even if some people are corrupt, how can the others accept it? Mercifully, a big wave did the needful and I was in the water. Cigar ruined and speechless, fumbling for the Italian version of touche.

GUNS AND LOSSES

MAHENDRA VED

SHE WAS LIVELY as Latinos are. Chic, cheeky and aggressive while arguing. New to Europe, we were learning to adjust to the new environment. She had three other Latin colleagues with whom she would burst into Spanish till she felt it necessary to move away from them. She preferred me to the Arabs and Africans who found her more talkative and with her Spanish accent, less comprehensible. The similarity in our complexions also mattered, I was to learn later. And I learnt it by silently paying her bills at the cafeteria many a time. "How do I know I should bill them separately? I thought they are husband and wife," the waiter explained to our escort. When it was translated to her, she blushed and then burst out laughing, "mira, mira, mira. Look at my husband."

This self-proclaimed, pint-sized revolutionary from Chile, then ruled by Salvador Allende, wanted to carry a gun and fight 'American imperialism'. "How would I look with a gun?" she asked me once, her eyes shining.

"It will have to be a very light gun for your delicate shoulders," I said.

She ignored the touch of romance in my voice and said, "I am very tough, you know."

She had one ambition — to meet Fidel Castro. Allende was of course a hero. But Castro was the inspiration. Santiago was in turmoil. Allende had already become the guy-who-must-go. Would she migrate to Cuba? No way. "Me and my Chile." But she promised to write to me the day her ambition to meet Castro was fulfilled.

By the time our training programme ended, to the envy of many, we had become close friends. She was in tears, and I, a few pegs down, sentimental, when we had the last dance. Nancy haunted me when I got back home. She hadn't given me her address, unsure of when she would go home, and under what conditions. For weeks, I longed for her letter.

Then, one day, the call of duty took me to Delhi airport. I was assigned to report the arrival of Castro. He was visiting India at the invitation of Indira Gandhi. The 'Big Cuban' broke protocol, ignored the police cordon and moved across to shake hands with one and all. I too extended mine, half his size. I thought of Nancy. Had I beaten the Latin lass at meeting Castro? On the way to office, I was thinking less of the news report on Castro's arrival and more about how I could get across to Nancy. In the office, the teleprinter at the foreign desk sounded the alarm, alerting us to a 'flash'. The news was from Santiago. The presidential palace had been stormed and Allende, it later turned out, had died fighting.

That was 27 years ago. In Santiago last week, thousands were on the streets remembering Allende and calling for the blood of Augusto Pinochet, his successor. Castro was at the United Nations, making a big splash and shaking hands with Bill Clinton. I haven't heard from Nancy. Did she get to shake hands with Castro?

BLACK BOOTY

SAAZ AGGARWAL

I WALKED THROUGH the door of my house, and nearly fainted at the words I heard blaring over the music system. Before I could wonder if I'd imagined them, there they came again, loud, cheerful and mellifluous: "I want to see your underwear..."

Until that moment two years ago, I had naively and somewhat egoistically imagined the generation gap to be a figment of fevered imaginations which, like Santa and time travel, simply did not exist, and if it did, merely represented the incompetencies of my own parents. Even more painful was the fact that none of my children were yet of an age to be interested in anyone else's underwear. It struck me that tastes in music define a generation as clearly as traits such as hard work, birth control, fondness for hashish or a facility with the newest technologies.

Another reminder of the generation gap came recently at the Black Country Museum in England. The Black Country, immortalized in print and celluloid by British media personality Meera Syal, is so named not for the numerous Indians who inhabit it but for its role in the Industrial Revolution. "Black by day and red by night, unmatched for vast and varied production, by any other space of equal radius on the surface of the globe," the American consul in Birmingham in 1868 declared.

The museum is set in a 26-acre site and recreates the living and working conditions of those days. We went down into a coal mine, took a ride on a canal boat, visited ironmongers, sweetshops and apothecaries, saw a silent movie in a shed-like hall, and even had a lesson in a Victorian classroom where the teacher wore a black gown, spoke in a shrill falsetto and kept a wooden cane at hand. Much that we saw, including the cinema, buildings and some products in the shops were familiar to me from my own childhood.

Tea-plantation bungalows and wooden-floored boarding school dormitories in the Nilgiris still retained much of the Victorian era a quarter century ago and perhaps still do. So, when we walked into a shop and one of my teenage daughters pointed at a bacon-slicing machine, saying, "That must be the photocopier," I was startled into a sudden clear vision of what a different world my children live in. By the time I dared to imagine such a miracle as a photocopier, I must have been in my twenties. For me the museum had been more about nostalgia than novel experience.

But in the end, the Black Country Museum presented us with an encounter which reassured us that the world is indeed a familiar and cozy sort of place. At the fossil and gift shop, there were beautiful stones on sale. When we told the man we collect stones like these from the ground around our house, he politely asked where we were from. We said, "Pune, India." He laughed, picked up one of the stones and showed us a label which said that it had been brought here from 'Pune, India'. So, of course, we promised to come back again soon, this time with a big boxfull of stones.

DOLLAR DEVOTEES

MALATHI RAMACHANDRAN

IN THIS ANCIENT land of a thousand and eight gods, there's a modern deity of formidable powers which has fought its way to the forefront of the pantheon. The Dollar God. While the devotees of yore stood patiently outside temples for hours just to get a *darshan* of the Lord, today's masses stand in snaking queues, battling sun and rain, just to gain entry into the US embassy. They don't wake up at the crack of dawn as their forefathers did, to bathe and offer prayers, but to make it to the top of the line. As the 'temple' doors are thrown open, there's an air of anticipation and anxiety, the closest of which emotions were once glimpsed only in Tirumala or Vaishnodevi as the *sanctum sanctorum* came into view. Hours later, these modern devotees emerge with the air of one who's glimpsed God, and clutching the precious *prasad* — a visa to the US of A.

This new cult cuts across all barriers — of age, sex and social standing. Today you don't have to be a doctor or engineer to set out across the seas in pursuit of this god. You just need to be desperate enough to get rich quick. *Maamis* from the South elbow their way into low-cost Emirates or Korean flights, side by side with red-lipped *bahenjis* from Punjab. Their dollar-eyed families bravely end them away to sales-counter jobs, also certain of winging it there once the cash registers (pun intended) start ringing. So what if they pay you only a fraction of what a resident American will get for the same job. Students scorn admissions in reputed Indian colleges for a place in even an unknown American university. Young men and women scan the matrimonial columns for green card-holders, not marriage partners. And couples delay their families till they are safely in the promised land. Try moving them out till they have had their 'American' child.

But the path of true devotion is never smooth. And this is a very demanding god. So our hopeful settlers rough it out in tenements or crowd in with distant family. They work long hours, eat plastic food from plastic containers and exclaim over the clockwork systems while turning into machines themselves. Wake up early, off to work, then turn in early, so as to wake up early again... the wheel grinds on. There's no time for family and friends, to lie about, to laze, to dream... But then, they're a part of the Great Indian Dream in America. Life is good, in fact, it's 'great'. Slowly, there's a house, two drawing rooms, two dining rooms, two TVs, two cars. They've arrived. A swimming pool in the backyard, and they've achieved nirvana. The Dollar God sure is good to his worshippers.

LINGERIE SURPRISE

DANNY TRAVASSO

EVER TRIED BUYING lingerie for the wife? If you have, you will probably agree that it is one of those tasks in life that rank under "things to be avoided at all costs," like crossing a busy road blind-folded. But sometimes, it can't be avoided. Like when there's a birthday coming up and you would like to really surprise her by gifting her the unexpected.

Walk into the store and be prepared for suspicious looks from the sales staff. The first thing you need to do — obviously — is to make sure you don't recognise anyone in the vicinity. Scrutinize all faces carefully and see if any match with known faces in your memory data bank. If so, turn around and leave. You can always buy the wife a goldfish instead. That way, you can survive to live another day with your dignity intact. After you get past this first obstacle your vision will be filled with a whole lot of lacy, frilly stuff, other stuff with straps and maybe buckles. The colour has probably drained from your face by now. Somehow, this isn't the same as watching the lovely ladies on Fashion TV back in the solitude of your room.

You shouldn't be surprised if the salesgirl gives you a hostile look. Here, it would help a lot if you were to put your hands on the counter. Besides steadying yourself for the ordeal ahead, you are also exhibiting your wedding ring boldly. She now knows you are a married man, which should help break down her wintry demeanour. And in matters like these, size does matter. Because if you don't know your wife's measurements in the various departments, you are like a deaf man attending a concert; you are lost. And of course, pointing at the salesgirl and saying: "She's about your size," is a bad move.

If the item of your choice is in the catalogue, your task is easier and you leave quickly. Otherwise, you are going to have the salesgirl staring at you while you try to describe what you want, hoping all the while that no one is around to overhear. By the time you get to the pay counter, your hands may be shaking.

Task accomplished you break into the open, a prisoner who's been set free. But when you reach home and the wife opens the gift and you see the smile on her face and the gleam in her eyes, that's when you feel that it was well worth the trouble.

THE LAST TAKE

ANAND KURIAN

SHE WAS WAIF-like when I met her for the first time. Most models are slim but the girl before me had an almost brittle fragility. Later I learnt that she was just 18; the Miss India crown had found her early. She was on her way to the Miss World finals and we were shooting a soap commercial for a multinational two days before she left. I was not happy with that — two days is too short to shoot such films.

The glowing skin takes make-up men and cinematographers many hours to create; the hair, the bane of all such shoots, could take far more. We had only two days nevertheless, and since I was just making my way in the advertising industry, I was in no position to put my foot down. She was all the things that she was said to be — professional and intelligent — but she had never performed before a camera.

Adrian, the creative chief of the agency, had added a small word to the script, *"Chhuoge?"* which roughly translated means, 'Would you like to touch me?' The line needed an innocent flirtatiousness. I am said to be good with amateurs, but in spite of take after take, the shot was not 'happening'.

Then some time before the end of the shoot, other problems cropped up. She said the beauty pageant organizers were screaming; she was to fly out that night, there were a hundred details to sort out. I had no alternative but to be cold-blooded. I had a job to do, I told her. The organizers screamed at her from the other end of the cellphone. They asked her to leave the set; I was equally firm. She burst into tears. Adrian and I flew to her side but even as we comforted her, my principal worry was that her tear-stained face would not show up well on camera. So we turned on our charm. And she proved to be made of sterner stuff than we thought, she wiped away her tears, took a deep breath. I called out 'camera, action' and she turned seductively to the camera and said with all the innocence of her 18 years, "*Chhuoge?*" You got it perfect in the last take on that day, Nafisa. If only the very last and final take hadn't gone so terribly wrong.

SWEET MELODY

JANARDHAN ROYE

SHE WAS MY childhood heart-throb and now an unexpected encounter was threatening to break my heart all over again. I was on a Mumbai-Delhi flight some years ago, and hardly took notice of the heavily made-up lady who was trying to squeeze her bulk past me to a seat next to mine. She seemed familiar.

I put the paper down when she addressed me to complain about the air hostess. I took a second dekko. Yes, it was she. The *sun, sun, sun zaalima...* lady from my movie-mad childhood days. She had my pubescent heart thumping wildly those days.

"Shyamaji," I said. Her anger with the air hostess subsided. She turned to me, "You recognize me?"

"How could I not?" I replied, hoping not to sound too filmy. As the jet got airborne, our conversation drifted to *Aar Paar* and Guru Dutt. She was delighted when I told her how ravishing she looked in the film. We stuck up a wonderful rapport.

"Yes, I enjoyed playing that role in *Aar Paar*. Then abruptly her mood changed. Tears welled up in her eyes. She said, "Okay, young man, let's see if you remember songs from the film," she teased, "Sing any song you like."

"Sing? Now?" I asked nervously, looking around.

"Yes, now," she laughed. Then started coughing. "This cough. They say it's got to do with my heart. *Toba*! Cough and heart, have you heard such nonsense? Now, sing!" It was a command.

Sun, sun, sun zaalima... is sung twice in the movie. The svelte

Shyama, bewitching in *dungarees*, sings the lively duet with Guru Dutt. Later, heart-broken she pines for her lover with the plaintive, *ja, ja bewafa...*

I began the slow version in a whisper. Not remembering all the words I went on, humming and ending with *preet re....* She was delighted with the effort. She knew the words and joined in. Her singing was strong and had a touching quality about it — until her cough got in the way. Before we knew it, the aircraft was ready to land. I watched helplessly as she coughed spasmodically. She waved me to get up and go. Whether it was emotion or just physical discomfort, I don't know. But apparently she didn't want me to see her like that. I stood by the aircraft door to watch the air hostess help her up. For the rest of that day *ja, ja, ja bewafaa,* took complete hold over me.

A BATTLE AND A SMILE

RAHUL SINGH

IN 1962, WHEN I was just 22 years old, I did something considered unusual at the time. Along with an English friend who had been at university with me, we decided to go overland by car from England to India. While traversing Italy, we came to a picturesque town called Monte Cassino. The town was on top of a towering cone of land, rising 5,000 feet above the Liri Valley.

In those days, I still had the outward symbols of a Sikh — beard, long hair and turban. While walking around Monte Cassino, an elderly lady who clearly spoke no English came up to me, pointed to my turban and gave me a beautiful, warm smile. Her animated talk made no sense to me. But the smile somehow conveyed more than just simple curiosity at seeing a Sikh. When other townspeople also did the same, I was intrigued. I got hold of somebody who could speak a little English. He explained that Monte Cassino had been the site of an epic battle in World War II, in which Sikh troops had played a prominent role. He told me that they remembered their great courage and sacrifice, with nostalgia and affection.

When I got back to India, I dug into some books on military history. One book described the battle of Monte Cassino "in the heroic category of Dunkirk and Stalingrad". Monte Cassino, the book said, was considered impregnable and the Germans were there in full force, hoping to halt and perhaps even beat back the Allied advance. The famed 15th Panzer Grenadier Division, tough veterans of a dozen battlefields, held the town. Hitler had sent the German commander, Major General Baade, a direct order that Monte Cassino must be held "whatever the cost". In one dispatch, the Germans referred to their adversaries as "Indian troops with turbans". They had obviously never encountered Sikhs before. Two fierce Allied assaults up the mountainside, lasting six bloody weeks, failed, the 4th Indian division losing 4,000 men. But the fury of those assaults had shaken the German troops. The 8th Indian division was moved up in support and it succeeded in smashing through the German defences and occupying the main commanding heights. The Germans had been defeated and the road to Rome was finally open.

All this took place almost exactly 60 years ago. Monte Cassino was one of the most glorious chapters in the history of the Indian army. But it was the warm smile of that Italian woman, who had seen it all, that made me realize it.

ALWAYS A GENTLEMAN

GAYATRI RAY

THOUGH HE WOULD have been 60 today, my mind flies back to a well-behaved, handsome boy of about 12, keeping an eye on a mischievous little brother while his grandfather and mother were busy with diplomatic engagements. The place was West Germany, and young Rajiv Gandhi was keeping a steady hand on his energetic brother Sanjay during prime minister Jawaharlal Nehru's visit, accompanied by Indira Gandhi, who was his official hostess at that time.

I had come to Bonn with my husband from the consulate in Berlin, as he was part of the Indian delegation. The Suez crisis loomed and the Soviet invasion of Hungary was imminent. Little did we know that the happy family tableau we were privy to that summer of 1956 was a rare event indeed — three prime ministers of India, enjoying precious moments amid the affairs of state. Especially the quiet, polite little boy with a shy smile. The schedule was tight, given the German penchant for work, but Chancellor Adenauer saw to it that Panditji's itinerary was enlivened by sightseeing tours so that the family could imbibe as much *frische luft* (fresh air) as possible. The highlight was a cruise down the Rhine, which got both the little boys very excited and young Rajiv had to keep a hold on his sibling as the boat sliced through deep waters.

I was to hear later that when the adults were busy and the lure of the unmanned elevator in the ambassador's residence proved irresistible, Rajiv politely checked his brother's enthusiasm. The household staff couldn't heap enough praise on the deportment of the elder boy. And my own observations only confirmed their assessment.

Two decades later I saw Rajiv Gandhi again, now as a young man concerned about his mother's safety after the Emergency was lifted. On the last day of electioneering in 1977, I saw him follow Indira Gandhi in a separate car to three successive meetings. Innate good manners made him refuse to take a prominent place in any of these functions.

Destiny, however, made Rajiv a reluctant player in the political arena soon after. Steeped as I was in diplomatic protocol, even I was amazed at the norms he set for treatment of visitors as AICC general secretary. He himself ushered me into his office and did not sit till I did. And when I was leaving he came right to the door to say goodbye. It was cruelly ironic that this quintessential *bhadralok's* life was snuffed out when he was courteously accepting a garland.

AN OLYMPIAN & A GENTLEMAN

PRIYADARSHI MITRA

"DEAR PRIYADARSHI, I wish I was there personally to thank you for the kind words and be with you at this moment of pride for our country and not writing a mail. I, too, am longing to meet you and we shall do so soon on my return. Please do convey my personal thanks and regards to uncle, Lily and Pritish for their best wishes. My mother is there in Delhi, so do give her a call. She will be delighted. Looking forward to meeting you. Chilly."

This was the reply to the mail I had sent Major Rajyavardhan Singh Rathore or Chilly, as he is affectionately called, after his win at Athens Olympics. Nowhere in the mail did he highlight his achievement. Rather he summed it up as a moment of pride for the country.

My association with Chilly goes back to the early nineties when my father who was in the army was posted in Jaipur. Chilly's father was also posted there. They stayed right opposite our house. I was chatting with a friend when Chilly came up to us and introduced himself. He had just been commissioned in the army. We chatted for a while and I found him to be straightforward and simple. We soon became friends and whenever he came on leave, we got together and chatted or played cricket. The driveway of their home used to be our playground. Once he had an accident and his foot was in plaster. It was then that I spent maximum time with him. Our colony was located near the polo grounds of the elite 61st Cavalry. We had quite a few celebrity polo players as our neighbours, such as Col R S 'Pickles' Sodhi, Col KS Garcha and Col RS Brar. I remember watching their polo matches with Chilly and discussing their celebrity status, never realizing that there was a budding celebrity amongst us.

After Jaipur I lost touch with him for a while but we resumed contact in 2002. By then he was a national figure in shooting. It did not come as a surprise that he had taken up shooting as a sport, for he always had a focused approach to life. Chilly believes that it's never too late to start something. After all he took up shooting at 28. Fame and success has not gone to his head. It proves that apart from being an officer and an Olympian he is a thorough gentleman.

ACTING MP

VN KAKAR

WHEN PRITHVIRAJ KAPOOR left Peshawar for Mumbai early last century, everybody told his mother that she had lost her son to sin. Mumbai in those days was known in Peshawar, my hometown, as the city of sin. No one could imagine then that Prithviraj's journey would result in the foundation of the famous Prithvi Theatre and see the emergence of the Kapoor clan in Bollywood. From Shashi, Shammi and Raj to Randhir, Kareena and Karisma and a host of others, Mumbai owes so much to Peshawar. Prithvi was followed by Yusuf Khan (Dileep Kumar), Zakiria Khan (Jayant), Amjad Khan's father, and several others, including theatre managers.

Jawaharlal Nehru was one of Prithvi's great admirers. He nominated him to the Rajya Sabha. And it was in that capacity that I ran into him in 1960 when he was staying at the erstwhile Constitution House on Kasturba Gandhi Marg in New Delhi. I, too, was allotted a room there on my first appointment in the government of India. Naturally I went to pay my respects to Prithviraj. We were sitting in the dining hall having lunch. I went up to him and told him that I, too, was from Peshawar. From then onwards, whenever he was in the dining hall, he would call me to his table and talk to me of days gone by.

"Shall I tell you something," he said once jocularly. "I really do not know what I am supposed to do in the Rajya Sabha. It was easier for me to act as Mughal-e-Azam in the film of that name than to play the role of an MP in the Rajya Sabha. God knows what Panditji saw in me. But whenever I am in Delhi and the Rajya Sabha is in session, I make it a point to attend it."

Prithviraj never allowed me to pay for my bills. He said to me bluntly that it would be highly impertinent on my part to pay for my meals when he was there. Once I had guests. He paid for them as well. "Your guests," said he, "are my guests," and then added laughing, "You know one thing, my dear boy, for your guests, you will have to pay Rs5 per head. If they are mine, I have to pay just Rs2.50. That is one of the many privileges I enjoy as an MP."

CAN'T HURRY LOVE

AVINASH S VAZ

SHE WAS CUTE and her soft spoken manner had made me fall head-over-heels in love with her. Though we were in the same class, in college for three years, all could do was to speak to her on a few occasions.

Finally it was the last day of college. A day when I would be meeting her probably for the last time It was this thought that propelled me to convey the message that had lingered in my heart for so long. Gathering enough courage I called out to her. She was walking towards the bus stand. "Hi! I want to tell you something," I said hiding my nervousness She paused for a while and then replied, "Hmmm... Okay, tell me what is it?" "Not here, if you don't mind, we could have something over there," I said pointing to a fast-food joint nearby. She looked at her watch and agreed. "The moment my bus comes I will be off," she added.

"What is it," she said after selecting a corner table. Her question was enough to stir butterflies in my stomach.

"What will you have?" I tried to avoid her question.

"A cola would do." The waiter was quick to honour the order.

"What is it?" she asked again looking at her watch.

"How did your exams go?" I asked.

"Think you have asked me this question earlier in the canteen and I think I have given you a suitable reply." That was enough to shut me up. My mind searched for words. I looked at my bottle and took a sip. She had almost finished, whereas getting a sip down my throat was proving difficult. The next few minutes were spent in silence.

I started to tell her about my holiday plans which she interrupted midway. “Have you called me here to discuss your holiday plans. Can you pass me a tissue?” she said. I immediately handed over the whole box to her. She picked out one and scribbled something “Read this fast. It’s time for my bus and I have to leave,” she picked up her bag without wasting time I read out “I love...” she stared at me trying to control her laughter. “By the way how was my acting? I knew you had a soft spot for me and you would say something on the last day,” she said. The bus stopped and honked as both of us continued laughing our hearts out.

EVERGREEN OPTIMISM

RAJIV DESAI

AS I STOOD there shaking hands with him when he came to receive the DadaSaheb Phalke award, the years seemed to melt away. It was as though I was in my pre-teens, having just watched *Nau Do Gyarah, Munimji, Paying Guest* or whichever film I first saw starring Dev Anand. I can remember going straight into the bath room, wetting my hair and trying to work up the stylish pompadour. Dev Anand was my absolute favourite screen personality and I religiously caught every single film he ever made.

My friends say I am an inveterate optimist, that's why I came back to India after nearly two decades in the US. The optimism has its roots in my early exposure to Dev Anand's films since the late 1950s and through the early 1960s; he was my favorite hero, not necessarily because he was a good actor but because he stood for hope. While Dilip Kumar represented the tragedy of the Indian condition, Raj Kapoor the misbegotten ideology that messed up India, Dev Anand stood for what India could be, smiling and stylish with a song on the lips.

Dev Anand represents the most modern of all creative idioms: Find talented people and let them grow. Through his organization, Navketan, we were introduced to Guru Dutt, SD Burman and dozens of others, who entertained generations with movies and music that today are part of our memories. About the time Dev Anand began to be recognized as an entertainer, the operative mood in Indian films was down-in-the mouth, a victim of the colonial experience. The theme song was *Duniya mein hum ayein hain to jeena hi padega, jeevan hai agar zahar to peena hi padega.* Along came Dev Anand with his worldview expressed best in the song from the film *Hum Dono: Barbadiyon ka shok manana fuzul tha, har fikr ko dhuein mein udata chala gaya.* His films filled me with hope, the ultimate global value that was in short supply in India at that time.

Congratulations on the Dadasaheb Phalke Award, and thank you Dev Saheb, you instilled me with optimism about India before I reached my teens. In the words of your immortal song: *Jeevan ke safar mein raahi... de jaate hain yaadein.* Indeed, you have given me, a fellow traveller in the world, a rich lode of memories, never mind your lyricist's other lines, which I have left out in the ellipsis.

HOSPITAL HUMOUR

NARENDRA NAIR

PEOPLE THINK THAT a hospital is a drab and miserable place. That, since patients come for a cure for their illnesses they generally have a bleak and dreary air about them. That, this then rubs off on to the doctors and nurses who as a consequence adopt a defensive brusqueness and bland exterior.

On the contrary, the hospital is often a place of great humour and lightheartedness, and human foibles get laughed at in much the same way as in other places. Over the past quarter of a century I have had a fair share of 'moments of mirth' and I have only been richer for the experience.

Hospital humour comes in a variety of shapes and sizes. I still remember our teacher in medical college chiding a freshman on poor history taking. The freshman had been assigned to a patient who had a peculiar bowel disturbance. The freshman had been, like all fellows new to the job, pretty direct in his questioning. He asked the patient what the problem was. The teacher broke in to tell him that this was not the way to obtain delicate personal information. The teacher volunteered to show us how to ask such questions and putting his hand on the patient's shoulder, gently enquired — "My dear man, do you have a problem with your toilet?" To which the patient nodded brightly and replied, "Yes sir. Thank you for asking. The roof leaks."

Another time, a villager from Uttar Pradesh came with a mass in his neck that had, as goiters tend to do in that part of the country, grown quite big. We wanted a clinical photograph of the thyroid swelling for our teaching files. The patient was accordingly told to come for his photograph the following day. He duly presented himself with wife and son in tow, in freshly laundered clothes and a generous amount of talcum powder applied to his face. He innocently explained to the surprized nurse that he did not want his picture taken alone and that he wished to include his family as well.

There are stories galore of how patients and doctors find humour a source of comfort in desperate situations. Like the patient who started auto-urine therapy for a highly invasive cancer, and when asked if he wasn't worried about bad breath, he explained that bad breath was better than no breath at all.

DORIS DAY SPECIAL

JANARDHAN ROYE

IT WAS 1981 and my first assignments in the USA. We were in a tiny airport in Kalamazoo, Mich, attired in jackets with briefcases in hand. It was a beautiful summer day and my colleague Hank was whistling "People will say we are in love."

We were greeted at the small aircraft by a large billowy blonde with sparkling blue eyes. After settling down comfortably in my seat I looked out besides the nine people inside, three women in business suits were running towards the aircraft below, our blonde hostess was counting and hoisting bags into the hold. A little later, she climbed in pulling up the boarding ladder. The aircraft engine continued to make a soft purring sound. The blonde did a brisk head count and then disappeared into the cabin. A few seconds later, at the time of departure, she was back, and spoke into a microphone.

"Good morning folks. I am Doris, your pilot. You are requested to have the safety belt on during the duration of the flight..." She went on to explain the safety and other precautions, ending with "presently, you will be served refreshments." She disappeared into the back of the aircraft and emerged with a large plastic bag from which she handed out packets of pretzels and orange juice. Having done that she said, "We will now take off. Relax and have a pleasant flight, folks." The small aircraft taxied down the tarmac, a bit bumpily and took off with a shudder. After some time, with the steady drone of the aircraft Hank closed his eyes. And before we knew it, our aircraft was descending the voice over the PA system said, "Please straighten your seats and fasten your seat belts, we're about to land." Then the plane did a perfect landing.

The blonde was back in front of us. "Was that a good flight or what?" she gushed, smiling broadly at the passengers. "You did just fine, Doris," said an uniformed man sitting in the last row. She paused to wave to him, "I hope you enjoyed the flight as much as I did. Gosh, this is the first time I have flown a plane alone."

Hank blinked several times, and his jaw dropped as the lady continued, "Now please remain seated I'll have the boarding ladder down momentarily. Then I'll get your bags." As Doris stood next to the baggage, smiling and bidding us goodbye, I couldn't help looking back and admiring this one-woman crew.

WORD POWER

A MADHAVAN

AFTER THREE YEARS I am still a computer novice. I use the wonder machine to less than 10 per cent of its capacity: for e-mails and thrifty browsing at a few sites on the Net. I have given a miss to spreadsheets, powerpoint, charts, graphs, tables, 'macros', mail merge, and other arcane rites dear to adepts. In the beginning was my 'word'; in the end also.

One of the gifts of word is ABC. It lives on the second toolbar. It is neither a new alphabet in fancy type, nor an acronym for 'absolutely bemused chump'. Its other name is 'spell check', a throw-back to a faultfinding pedant of a schoolteacher who constantly carped at your errors in spelling and grammar.

ABC loves to underscore your copy in red and green wavy lines, drawing attention to your solecisms, real and alleged. Green for grammar, red for spelling. It will pounce on any misplaced comma, unclosed quotation marks or verb less sentence, such as the last one. It is allergic to the passive voice, even when it is used to stress the act rather than the agent. It dislikes sentences longer than three lines. ABC provides an option for American or British spelling. This is handy for typing the '-ize' verbs with out irritation. It magnanimously lets you ignore its presumptuous recommendations. You can even banish it altogether if you risk your writing to go out with no in dependent proof-reading.

I have mixed feelings about ABC's critical attentions. I like its kingfisher quick darts at typos on the screen. But it can be obtuse after all, you are smarter than a software programme. It can't tell if word, correctly spelt, is obviously a misfit in the text. For example, if I had typed 'spilt' instead of 'spelt' in the last sentence, it has raised no objection. It is sometimes contradictory. If you type 'southwest monsoon, it will react with 'south-west'. OK, you say have it your own way, and correct it to 'south-west Perversely it prefers 'south west' this time. Try it with 'standoff'. I'm afraid this hyphen dilemma will make it self-destruct in smoke.

ABC can be unintentionally hilarious with words and names not in its lexicon. 'Bangalore' prompts 'bungler'. 'Kannada' suggests 'canned'. 'Deccan' triggers 'decay', 'Bihar' 'bizarre', 'Shimla' 'shambles'. 'Lakh' is a mistake 'lake', it believes, and 'crore' must be 'crone'. 'Pandit Nehru' emerges from coils as 'bandit negro'.

UP IN SMOKE

RAJ CHATTERJEE

THIS SCARE, BEGUN in the West, and now taken up vigorously by us, about the harmful effects of smoking reminds me of what Leo Tolstoy wrote a long time ago in one of his essays. Tolstoy equated the smoking habit with an indulgence in "vodka, wine, beer, opium, hashish and fly-agaric (whatever that may be)". "We are addicted to these things", he said, because of our dual personalities. Each one of us is a combination of two different beings; the one blind and physical; the other, seeing and spiritual. The one eats, drinks, smokes, sleeps, propagates; the other merely appraises the activities of the former. It is, in fact, that rather troublesome person — the conscience."

According to Tolstoy, when we indulge in one or more of the 'stupifires' listed above, we are really trying to dull our conscience and pander to our appetites, inherited or acquired. Many of us will not agree with this view. However, to quote Tolstoy, "Everybody knows by experience that a man's frame of mind is altered by the use of wine or tobacco, that he is not ashamed of things which but for the stimulant he would be ashamed of."

Tolstoy proceeds to ridicule the popular 'fallacies' that smoking helps to pass the time, cheers one up and is conducive to clear thinking. On the contrary, amongst the votaries of the fragrant weed he numbers boys who have learnt the "facts of life" and "libertines, gamblers, ladies of easy virtue and lunatics". So, we really have three distinct relationships — between smoking and lung cancer, between smoking and cardio-vascular diseases and between smoking and loose living. Cigarette prices being what they are today, I should like to add a fourth correlation, between smoking and penury.

In fact, Tolstoy himself in the same essay, mentions another relationship which should be of interest to our authors and journalists. Let them not put forward the excuse that they are unable to concentrate on their tasks unless they are blowing clouds of smoke to add to the pollution in the air. In each one of them, says Tolstoy, there are two distinct beings, the writer and the critic. When the former pulls at a cigarette he is merely trying to dull the sensibilities of the latter so that he will pass the indifferent work that he reviews.

Let our leader-writers not forget that their penmanship will be appraised by thousands of people who neither smoke nor drink, that thousands more will be driven to abstention not so much by the statistics produced by medical researchers or anti-pollution propagandists, as by the budgets presented by our finance ministers each year.

DOUBLE STANDARDS

MAYAH BALSE

SOME MONTHS AGO, on a pleasant morning, I was reading the newspaper in the verandah when I heard a peculiar ring. It was not the door bell. Nor was it the intercom. Not the landline either. What was it? Was my hearing beginning to fail? Just then my maid called me from the kitchen and that solved the mystery. It was her mobile phone. Her hands were full of dough as she was kneading *atta*, so she asked me to put the instrument to her ear.

Her conversation over, I retreated back to my favourite armchair with the newspaper. Five minutes later she came and stood beside me. She wanted a loan of five thousand rupees. It was for roof repairs, she said. I pointed out that the monsoon was not due for some time. "Suppose the roof falls on our head?" She had a point. I gave her the money. Two months later she came to me happily and announced that she was going to acquire a new flat. A new flat in Mumbai? I was aghast. It had taken me a lifetime to save for one.

"Yes," she said happily. "I lied to you. The five thousand rupees was not for roof repairs. It was to bribe my way to get a certificate entitling me to a new house in the slum development project for huts built before 1995. Mine was built later, so I wouldn't have got a free flat."

I pointed out the evils of bribing. She told me with a straight face that ministers, top officials and even the police did it. The whole nation did it. Why was I picking on her? I let it pass, but frowned with anger. She tried to placate me.

"I am doing it for my son," she said. "He is no good in academics. At least if he lives in a flat, he will get a girl with decent dowry." From bad to worse I thought. I kept mum, not wanting to launch into a discourse on the evils of dowry.

The story has a twist however. Few months later she came to me in tears. The municipal authorities had demolished her hut. "You had paid for the certificate entitling you to a new flat. You don't have to worry," I said.

"Certificate?" she cried. "It was a fake." And she spat an unprintable swear word and said, "Shame on those disgusting people who are ruining our country with corruption."

AN OLD FRIEND

NIRUPAMA SUBRAMANIAN

EVER SINCE I moved to Mumbai I had wanted to visit the city's bookshops. So one day I caught a local train and made the journey from the suburbs to town with a thrill of anticipation.

On the edge of the road, leading from Churchgate to Fort, I located the row of bookstalls. There were really only books stacked on the pavement. There were mostly second-hand books, which had passed from reader to reader till they had reached these stalls. There were some school textbooks stacked haphazardly in a corner. I could make out the title of one of them — *Introductory Chemistry*. I had studied a similar book during my school days. The cover was shiny blue when I had bought it but this book had a dull grey one. The design on the cover was however the same.

I had never enjoyed chemistry. The chemical formulae would spin dizzily around in my head and I could rarely balance any of the balancing equations. I remember dazed nights spent trying to memorize the periodic tables and the right alphanumeric combination to put around little hexagons.

However, there was something mystifying about the subject. I remembered the wonder of chemical reactions, the smell and sights of the laboratory sessions. I recall the sight of potassium permanganate crystals, lying on my palm, pink and glittering like fairy food, or the deep copper sulphate blue sediment in the test-tube which gleamed like a glorious Mediterranean sky. Sometimes I would feel like a magician creating the vivid orange-red flame of calcium oxide from two dull powders or a witch calling forth spirits through some unexpected white fumes. Once I had kept my chemistry book too close to the Bunsen burner and it had caught fire creating confusion and excitement during a dreary session. The book was not damaged except for a few singed margins of the back pages.

As I looked through the book, it seemed like discovering an old friend again. I turned to the first page to see the name of the owner. There were about three names that had been blackened out with ink to erase all previous claims to the book. I quickly skimmed through the pages. I then saw my name on page 22 — in school we used to write our names on the pages that corresponded to our birthdays. It was my handwriting, more rounded with my old signature. I surprized the shopkeeper by paying the Rs50 he asked for the book, without bargaining.

TO DIE FOR

VANDANA KUMARI JENA

IT WAS A bright summer morning when I received a disturbing email. My son studying near Chicago, had gone skydiving. For a moment my heart stopped, "What if?" the question swam before my eyes. Instantly I was on the phone and my son assuaged my fears.

"There were 12 of us," he said. Is there safety in numbers? "Prakrit," I said agitatedly, "If God wanted you to fly he would have given you wings."

"Mom," he retorted, "God must have skydived." "Nothing," he marvelled, "can quite capture the thrill. Nothing compares with the exultation of floating like a bird after the parachute has opened, the floating sensation which a sparrow, a seagull must feel while flying."

"Enough," I told my first born, "this madness must not be repeated."

"Once," he argued, "is not enough. Don't worry Ma during the first two jumps the instructor is there with me."

I was not placated. There was no mention of skydiving from him subsequently. I hoped and prayed that this was a closed chapter. On the day he had threatened to dive again, I lacked the courage to ring him up and ask him if he had gone skydiving. Instead I silently fretted at the thought of his jumping from a height of 14,000 feet. I finally picked up courage in the evening to call him. He hadn't been for his dive, his plans had been deferred he said. I heaved a sigh of relief and sent up a silent prayer. It was many days later that I discovered the reason for the deferment. My younger son let it slip out inadvertently. Prakrit, he informed us, didn't jump because his instructor died just a few days earlier.

"Hope," I said, my mind in turmoil, "not while skydiving." He acknowledged that this was indeed what had happened. The instructor, a veteran of 3,000 dives, had jumped with a friend, hand in hand. But the friend had been unable to time the opening of his parachute correctly, and fell on the instructor whose parachute collapsed. The instructor plummeted down from thousands of feet and died instantaneously. His friend fell on top of him and suffered broken bones. Prakrit though shaken by the tragedy did not want to show it. "So what Ma, he died doing what he loved best," said he.

I thought over what my son had said. I agreed with him that his instructor loved skydiving. But, I wondered though, was it something he was willing to die for?

AN OFFICER AND A SIREN

MN BATRA

MANSUR KHAN — MK for short — was a Pathan from Peshawar. His physique and good looks were somewhat like cricketer Imran Khan. MK was a good squash player and was popular socially. We first met in the office of Major MS Wadalia who was responsible for training at HQ Persia and Iraq Command located in Baghdad during World War II. At that time both of us were captains and had been selected to attend the Staff College course near Jerusalem in Palestine (now Israel).

There was no air service at that time so we travelled by civil bus across the desert from Baghdad to Damascus, which took 24 hours. Then across two cedar-covered mountain ranges to Beirut where we checked in at the famous Normandie hotel. For fear of German air-raids, there was complete black-out in Beirut after dark. Later, at dinner, MK gave me a nudge. "Look at the girl entering on your left. What a beauty," he exclaimed. Fascinated, we watched every move of this well-groomed Lebanese girl as she sat down a few tables away, studied the menu and ordered her meal in French.

"Forget about her," I said, "she probably belongs to the smart set." My comment seemed to stir up MK's Pathan blood and he swore in Pushto and Punjabi that he would meet her. We gathered as much information about the person and a suitably worded note was sent to her. An anxious wait and the bellhop appeared with an envelope what looked like book. The two-page reply was in French and the 'book' was a French English dictionary. Half an hour's labour on my part showed the answer to be a polite regret.

In the middle of that night, I woke up to the wail of air-raid siren. There was no sign of MK. I dashed out to find panic-stricken guests, in various stages of undress, rushing down to the basement shelters. Just as the siren stopped, I was flabbergasted to see MK walking down to the basement, carrying the Lebanese girl in his arms.

"How the hell did you do it?" I asked MK when the excitement was over and we were back in the room. "No problem," he answered nonchalantly, "the nearest air-raid warden was most cooperative — for a consideration, of course. A practice alert was sounded at a predetermined time when I just happened to be outside the girl's room. She shouted for help and, like a gallant army officer, I was there at moment's notice."

TAILORED MEMORIES

RUHI AMLE

HE WOULD NEVER tell us his name. When we tried guessing it, he would laugh and say, "I have no name." Tell us about your childhood, we'd pester. "I don't remember," he'd reply. He was from Margao and so everyone simply called him Margaokar.

As children, our clothes, from bloomers to frocks were stitched by Margaokar. All the Goan women in Pune camp, first generation immigrants from newly independent Goa, swore by him. They purchased fabrics in bits and pieces round the year and twice a year — before Christmas and before the annual summer exodus to Goa, Margaokar would be sent for.

Margaokar lived at the 'club'. This was actually an old house leased by some Goan bachelors who had come to Pune looking for jobs. It was not easy to engage him. Bookings had to be made weeks in advance. When Margaokar received my mother's summons, he would let her know the days when he would visit and mother would adjust all family matters, no matter how urgent, accordingly. Before his arrival our hand-sewing machine would be cleaned and oiled, threads and needles purchased. Most important of all, arrangements would be made for a supply of fresh fish and tiny yellow bananas, which with endless mugs of sweet, black tea were Margaokar's staple diet.

We would cluster around him as he arrived on his bicycle waiting impatiently while he removed his trouser-clips. He would then dig into his pockets for a packet of peppermints. While mother murmured, "Oh no, why do you bother...," we would pounce on them as if we had never seen a mint in our lives. Margaokar had a high nervous laugh, which peppered his non-stop conversation. After drinking his first cup of tea, he would take off his shirt and trousers and clad in a singlet and knee-length shorts, he would begin work. The machine would hum a background score for his continuous chatter and bursts of laughter as he recounted for mother's benefit all the events that had transpired in the families he had visited. Mother enjoyed his visits thoroughly.

As we grew older, we refused to wear clothes stitched by him. Margaokar was ageing. He could not cut patterns and set seams the way he used to. Somehow, Margaokar slipped out of our lives. Occasionally we heard snippets of news: Margaokar was ill..., the 'club' had been pulled down. This nameless tailor today is an integral part of my memories.

AAMCHI MUMBAI & I

DEEPALI PANT JOSHI

LIKE ANY OTHER migrant in search of new opportunities I came to meet you alone. The fearsome monsoon had just broken; grey clouds were hanging low over the Arabian Sea, buffeted by sheets of rain. Unnerved by the aggressive winds I stood trembling outside the imposing RBI building.

Today, as I bid adieu, I explore again the 'Internalities and Externalities of memory'. The Gothic columns of the Asiatic Library, the spectacular buildings in the Fort area. The impossible sophistication of NCPA where I enjoyed so many theatre performances, the Nehru Centre with its classical music concerts, the old lady of Boribunder.

The sweep of tall skyscrapers and wide roads fringed by palm trees which bent with the wind, teaching lessons of resilience and flexibility. The double-decker BEST bus whose stairs I eagerly clambered up to take in the sights of Mumbai. The Amul hoarding by Wilson College that always brought a smile to the lips, the familiar press of the surging crowds at Church gate station. The narrow third seat on the local train valiantly fought for, triumphantly acquired. Abrasive aggressive, in *yer fayce* Mumbai.

The Jehangir Art Gallery, the State Bank of India building and the canteen close by which offered affordable fare, the amazing street fare, *bhelpuri* and *vada pav.* The joy of reading *Bombay Times* with its Page 3 people one would never meet but who seemed like old friends. The Strand bookstore where one could browse for hours. And just when a book was longingly but firmly put down from nowhere, Mr. Shanbagh would materialize magically, at one's elbow with a special price. Not to forget the joys of trawling the book-lined pavements at Fountain, where one could watch the world go by.

And wherever I chose to go, there was always my friend, the sea, oh, I loved her, in all her moods, but especially in the monsoon when violent and enraged she splattered Worli sea face with walls of sea spray. My friends are all lost, some passed away, some moved away, there were many whose names I never found out, though we took the train together, or met in the lift, every day.

Like every migrant, I promise myself, some day I will return. I may, perhaps, return sometime, but even so, I know, "that one cannot step into the same river twice." You seduced me steadily, O Mumbai, with your glamour and bright lights. City of dreams, tinsel town, I pay tribute to you. Today, I say good-bye with a heavy heart.

A GOOD FRIEND

NAZIA MALLICK

"A GOOD BOOK is like a good friend, it will never let you down," said my mother, who was a voracious reader herself. Years later, I can vouch for this. Looking back, I recall how all of us at home read a lot. Our house used to be littered with books; 30 years ago there weren't many distractions.

War and Peace was the first book I picked up to read. Despite pouring over it for hours, I could not decipher it. I gave up realizing that I was being too ambitious for a 12-year-old. When I started reading *Dracula*, the elders at home tried to charm as well as warn me out of reading it. But on a winter night, I snuggled under the quilt reading the forbidden book using a torch. So wrapped up was I, that I did not realize that someone had lifted the quilt. It was my mother: "You will ruin your eyes."

Mother quietly took the torch and the book away, leaving me sleepless with a yearning to read the book. However, *Dracula* appeared less diabolic in broad daylight, when I was handed the book, with a chiding to be more selective in my readings.

Nothing could keep me away from the glorious world of black and white. During summer afternoons, I would find, on the terrace, a shady corner near the water tank and give in to the unbridled joy of reading whatever I could get hold of. However, on one such blissful afternoon when I was 'discovered' with a book which dealt with the murky world of the Mumbai film industry; my days of hiding were put to an end. And from then on my erratic selections and disordered passion was regimented and channelled into 'cultivated' ones like the classics. Those days, the only thing that made me study day and night for my exams, was the promise of books, a sackful of them, selected and specially ordered for me. The brown unopened sack kept in a corner used to propel me to put all my energy in getting good grades, failing which I would have never got to open that bagful of dreams.

And, many decades later, this is one passion which is still going strong. For me, books are the silent counselor and beacon of light in the storms of life. I read to forget, to bring back memories, to connect, to detach, to learn, to rejuvenate and to resurrect.

THE LAST OUTPOST

MUKTA MANI PUNJ

I WAS AN outspoken critic of the Raj throughout my school and college days. It was fate's way of shutting me up when I got married to a railway officer. Indian Railways, jokingly called by me "the last outpost of the British" promptly introduced me to the memsahib culture. Railway clubs with sahibs nursing their drinks, and the primand-propah ladies bragging about their kids' academic achievements, huge bungalows, government vehicles and outhouses — the *gora* sahib's term for servant accommodation. All bungalows had at least two and if one was lucky, even four or five of them.

My favourite posting was Raipur, in what was then undivided Madhya Pradesh. We were newly married and it had taken my husband about an hour to show me the bungalow and the land around it. Wide-eyed, I had taken in the acres of the vegetable garden, the lush lawns in the front and the badminton court at the side.

Like a proud general, I had daily presided over an army of five house helps. Now this is a luxury which, any woman would die for. Just imagine having two attendants, a gardener, a cook and a driver at your beck and call, 24 hours of the day and free of cost. How's that for paradise? My 'socialist' friends glared at what they called "blatant exploitation of the masses" but nonetheless didn't hesitate to borrow my cook or gardener for a day.

When it came to servants and attendants, my husband's next

posting in the Kharagpur Railway Depot seemed to follow the dictum — the more, the merrier. There apart from the usual slew of servants, I enjoyed the services of an exclusive *dhobi*, our very own *rickshaw wallah* and believe-it-or-not, a fly-boy whose only job was to exterminate any flies or mosquitoes daring to venture inside the bungalow.

Having made me a thorough and unashamed slave of such colossal luxury for 15 years, it came as a brutal shock to me when my husband announced his decision of taking premature retirement in order to start a business with a friend. My teenage son, aiming for the Harvard Business School, let out a whoop of joy while my discerning daughter silently slid close to me and gently stroked my trembling, well-manicured hands. Perhaps she understood, for she said, "Look at it this way mama — the last outpost of the British Raj just fell."

GLOBAL CITIZEN

KV KRISHNAN

"SO YOU ARE an Indian working in Bangkok for a project in Israel, employed by a US firm?" asked the burly man seated on a soggy *charpoy*. I was in a godforsaken 'interrogation room' in Colombo, staring back incredulously at this query. My situation did seem to warrant such an odd question.

Over the years, I have brooded over this episode. It saddens me to think that we so easily miss that sense of belonging to the world — which to me always seems like one big place. I guess, years of lugging suitcases along strange airports makes you look at this world very differently.

Over time you tend to eye the crowded lanes of Kolkata or Mumbai with the same sense of belonging as you would the bustling streets of Athens. As I would spend lazy evenings wandering along Tel Aviv beaches or driving by the hustle of the Ramallah dirt roads, I would see the same sights — of families lost in happiness or strife of their lives. The Israeli cabbie would often hum strains of *Awara hoon*, just as Jordanian immigration officials would make kind enquiries about Amitabh Bachchan's latest hits.

Many of our lives are so interwoven with that singular thread of humanity which we have often come to secretly accept but not admit. A Jewish acquaintance I was with, was reminiscing a strange story. About 20 years ago, an orthodox Israeli father was hurriedly driving a cherubic seven-year-old girl not far from the 'dangerous' streets of a nearby Palestinian stronghold. It wasn't unusual to hear the frequent staccato of gunfire even as Israeli guards would open fire retaliating to fiery Palestinian bombs that would rumble in the quiet of the desert. The little girl, with the friskiness of her age, opened the passenger door and was suddenly thrown out on the dirt road. A panic-stricken father, fearing the worst, watched helplessly as an old man across the street cradled the injured girl upon his shoulders and took her to his dirty hovel.

The penurious man tended to her miraculously minor scrapes with the choicest medicines from his closet, and then carefully handed her back to her relieved father. The girl — now my acquaintance — recounted between sobs that the old man was a Palestinian Arab killed by a stray bullet just two months after this act of kindness.

GAME OF THE NAME

INDU SARAIYA

GRAMMAR AND HISTORY conspire to impale in our minds characters like William the Conqueror, Attila the Hun, Alexander the Great, Ivan the Terrible, Aurangzeb 'Alamgir', Mahatma Gandhi, Aftab-e-Musiqui Ustad Faiyaz Khan, and numerous others — all persons who acquired their appellation; but the Indian woman, with little grammar and less history, is to her aliases born.

The last in an eight-member family, I collected an impressive number of sobriquets as I went along — 'Baby' to *Fui*, to *Maasi*, to *Bhabhi*, to *Jethani*, to *Derani*, to Mummy, to *Naani*, to *Kaki*. Each new relationship etched in a fullness here, a richness there. Each time I felt like a born-again clan member. There is nothing in the West that compares with this emotional network of suffixes, theirs barely going beyond the prosaic Grandpa, Grandma, Uncle, Aunt, in-laws, first cousin, second cousin, third cousin and so on *ad nauseum*.

The extended family spirit frequently spills over into one's neighbourhood. The friendly local vegetable vendor addresses you as Bhabhi; the odd day when he substitutes this with Madam he makes me wince. The passing stranger, asking you the whereabouts of a neighbourhood building, addresses you as Sister in a literal translation of the respectful *Bahen*. The taxi-driver, mindful of your greying hair and advancing age, addresses you with utmost concern (yes, this happens too) as *Maaji* or *Mataji*. The woman cow-keeper on the pavement wishes me every morning with "*Namaste, Bai.*"

However, the word *Bai* is a potential 'explosive.' Whereas in Maharashtra, I believe, it is just a suffix covering a wide range of women, from matrons to lady-employers down the line to the domestic dogsbody, in some North Indian states, the word has rather dubious connotations.

On one occasion this ambiguity led to an ugly situation. An unsuspecting Bambaiya domestic addressed his North Indian lady-employer as *Bai*; the lady — a lady after all — understood the communication glitch as something she'd have to put up with while living in Mumbai, but the husband who overheard the servant, rushed in a towering rage and sacked the poor fellow on the spot. Vocatives for me at home have varied over the years, chameleon-like, according to the region from which domestics hail — from *Bai*, to *Bahen*, to *Bhabhi*, to *Didi*, to *Amma*, to Auntie, to *Bibiji*, to the horrendous but safely neutral Memsaab.

And haven't you also been involved in social situations in which men hesitate to address you by your first name because that would be too familiar, or to address you as Mrs So-and-So because that would be too formal? They end up addressing you as "Er..." or "Ahem..." or "I say..." or just with a needless clearing of the throat. The source of so much mutuality and amusement, can woman be dubbed "God's second blunder," as Nietzsche famously averred?

RELATIVE IMPORTANCE

MITA GHOSE

WHEN I BEGAN my initial forays into freelance writing, I was an innocent venturing into unknown territory. Little did I know then, that the experience would leave me vulnerable, once more, to the highs and lows of adolescence — acute anxiety, inexplicable euphoria or deep disappointment, all remote-controlled by an invisible editor endowed with seemingly magical powers to single out my article. For publication or for the waste-paper basket.

The absence of my much-anticipated byline from the day's newspaper, made me as unreasonably resentful as a thwarted teenager. But my efforts to conceal my feelings never managed to deceive my father, who sought to console me in his unique manner.

"Never mind," he would declare breezily, when another writer's article usurped the column I had come to regard as my very own, "this moron is obviously related to the editor." Father's tongue-in-cheek explanation soon became a standing joke between us, acquiring with time, new dimensions of irreverence and its fleeting reward — shared hilarity. When, for instance, the same writer's byline appeared more than once a month, father automatically conferred on him the status of the editor's brother-in-law. With connotations in Bengali other than its literal one, the term was open to abuse, as it were, lending father's insinuations greater poignancy and leading, therefore, to further outbursts of mirth. However, as the writers so described, often belonged to different communities, I couldn't hold back the wry comment, that to accommodate the plethora of brothers-in-law father insisted on foisting on the poor man, the editor was left with no choice but to embrace polygamy.

Father, firm in his assumptions, allowed the fair sex no respite either. If the writer was a woman, she had to be either the editor's wife, his girlfriend or his sister-in-law. The claims of these three ladies, he explained with an arch look in mother's direction, could never be denied by a mere mortal, if he knew what was good for him. And was an editor anything more than that?

Subsequently, when my own articles were featured twice in the same month, I asked father innocently, what description, in terms of his criteria for judgment, could best fit the nature of my assumed relationship with the editor. Being neither wife, nor sister-in-law, nor even girl-friend, my identity vis-a-vis the all-powerful man, was open to decidedly sinister interpretations, wasn't it? Father's response, this time, was a sheepish grin. But I ought to have known that on this matter, he had reserved for himself, the last word.

One busy morning, catching him glance through the day's newspaper, I dared to borrow the derogatory term that had become his exclusive trademark for describing all contributors to the newspaper other than his beloved daughter and enquired casually: "So, which lucky moron's article is featured today?" Father turned to the relevant column and as he scanned it, a naughty smile illuminated his face. "The luckiest of them all," he replied, holding up the page to me. The byline which was clearly visible, robbed me of a ready repartee. It was my own.

UNTO THE LAST

RAJ CHATTERJEE

IT WAS QUIET. The shadows on the clipped lawn lay long and still and the air was heavy with the scent of jasmine. The house that stood at the end of the gravelled drive was solidly built. Despite the large number of windows it bore no resemblance to the typical inverted shoe-boxes of today in which the small quantity of actual masonary looks like strips of adhesive tape designed merely to support the large window frames.

I pressed the bell. A bearded man appeared, looking as if he had stepped out of a book about India by Kipling or EM Forster. He wore spotlessly white salwars and an achkan. On his head was a turban, also white, whose starched end stood up boldly. He salaamed me respectfully and motioned me to a chair. He switched on a ceiling fan and asked me if I would like a cold drink which I declined. His mistress, he said, was expecting me and would be out presently. She was feeding her dog at the moment. And then the lady of the house came out to the verandah followed by a black labrador whose shining coat told me that much care had been bestowed on him. The lady must have been in her seventies but she walked with a firm step. Her hair was snow-white but her wrinkled face could not hide its serene beauty.

"You have come in answer to my advertisement?" she said, as we both sat down. "Well, here's the dog. He is just 10 years old as I said in the advertisement, and he has been my closest companion since my husband died five years ago. I could have him put to asleep but I haven't the heart to do it. So I'm looking for someone who will be kind to him in his last few years. Your's was the only offer I received. People must have been put off by his age."

I patted the dog's head and he licked my hand. I asked the lady why she was giving him away. "I am going away," she said, "perhaps for a long time and I have no children to whom I could hand over the dog."

I said that my wife and I would do our utmost to provide a happy home for her dog. It was arranged that I would pick him up in 10 days' time. When I went to the house again I was struck by its forlorn look. No doors or windows were open but when I rang the bell the old retainer came out and salaamed me as he had one before. His face, I noticed, bore a look of intense sorrow. Before I could open my mouth he said that his mistress had died in her sleep just a couple of days after I had seen her. The doctor said that she had suffered a massive heart attack. Completely taken aback, I asked him about the dog.

"He died too," said the man. "He kept howling and didn't touch his food for three days. On the fourth day I found him lying dead on his cot in the memsahib's room."

MAKER OF MALGUDI

RAJNISH WATTAS

DEAR Mr RK Narayan,

On behalf of the residents of Malgudi please accept our heartiest congratulations on being conferred the Padma Vibhushan on the 51st Republic Day. In order to honour you suitably, we have planned a large public function in the maidan on Kabir Street, near the Sarayu.

The function to be presided over by the town's municipal commissioner is organized by Mr Sampath of Truth Printing Press, who shall also be publishing free leaflets and invitation cards for the occasion. Jagan, the miserly vendor of sweets, has decided to distribute free sweets to everyone on that day.

The Banner will carry public notices of the function. The headmaster of Albert Mission High School has declared a holiday to enable students to attend the big event. However, Swami and friends have other plans. They have fixed a cricket match with the MCC team of Lawley Extension. A few other attractions which may induce you to visit Malgudi are that Selvi, the famous dancer of the town, has offered to perform at the end of the function, while Sunrise Film Studios have decided to make a film on your life and times.

As somnolent Malgudi gets charged up with excitement over your visit, the talkative man, as usual hanging around at the Regal Haircutting Saloon, has spread wild rumours that you are unlikely to attend the function because of your present reclusive life and lack of interest in the goings-on at Malgudi.

May I, sir, on behalf of the organizing committee, beseech you, not to abandon us; for you are our maker and have given breath to our lives. It's not for nothing that people from all over the world read, talk and wonder about us. And some intrepid academicians even draw maps of the town, hold highbrow literary seminars about it and even manage to earn PhDs through this endearing pursuit.

Moreover, life has moved on in Malgudi too. Here is an update: Nagaraja has finally finished his epic on the sage Narada, which is being published by Truth Printing on offset press. It is slated for release by you at the function. Boeing Silk Sari Store has grown into a hopping mall where customers can now pay through credit cards and even order through the Internet. Market Road has been renamed after the current municipal commissioner, who was jailed under TADA but is now out on bail. The Sarayu riverside now boasts of many new resorts and hotels, thereby hiding the old dilapidated temple. Even the wild growth of the Mempi forests has been cleared to make way for new multistoreyed apartment blocks and factories. In the process, the scourge of tigers, or taxidermists like Vasu, ever inhabiting Malgudi again has been eliminated.

Therefore, we do hope, sir, that the changing face of modern Malgudi will interest you even more and further inspire your Muse. But, whatever else may change, may the master storyteller in you go on and on — about his Malgudi; which is everywhere and yet nowhere.

KNITTY-GRITTY

SAAZ AGGARWAL

I LEARNT TO knit when I was only six. But, unlike *taiji* who shares the same distinction, I was not married off shortly thereafter. My introduction to this fine if sturdy art happened during a brief and utterly desolate period of life in the boarding at Nazareth Convent, (yes, the very same Nazareth Convent immortalised in the Booker Prize-winning *God of Small Things*). Everyone else in Std III was learning to knit during their spare time and so did I.

Knitting, I've heard recently, can serve as excellent therapy. Some teach it to convicts and other anti-social elements in the hope of calming them down. My mother was a committed knitter. Not so much to keep her on the straight and narrow but as occupation for the long winter evenings. This was decades before TV came to our remote corner of the planet.

So knitting became part of my adolescent angst. I was bitterly disgusted by people who said, "Oh isn't that sweet, she's just like her mother" when our every social call would be interspersed with the speedy clickety-clack of both pairs of our knitting needles, and I longed to stab them between stitches. If my mother was a better, and more experienced, knitter than I, it was surely more coincidence. It was coincidence too that, 20 years later, the older women in my husband's family turned out to be great knitters. This gave us at least one major binding force, and the wool market in Delhi, with acres and acres of brilliant bales and loops of wool, was practically on the doorstep of the ancestral home. Over the years, various metaphors and cliches of knitting emerged.

Firstly, knitting, for all my youth and energy, was something only tired old women did. If at all a young woman knitted, it could only mean that 'good news' was on the way. I was acutely aware that knitting needless could be used for purposes of excavation when 'good news' was actually not good news but very, very bad news indeed; as, for example, in the case of Noelle in *The Other Side of Midnight*. Knitting was also the embodiment of patience and I owe it my ability for perseverance and mindless hard work.

Today, knitting is a dying art, a pastime of the previous millennium. Both my daughters were duly taught, and so was my son, on grounds of gender equality. But none has taken to it the way one might expect. To them, cable only means cable TV, and filet has to do with meat rather than needlework; they know nothing of jacquard, aran, and other bywords of my world. Yarn shops have closed down the world over, replaced by burger joints and gymnasiums.

But I have kept on knitting, even during the several years when I lived in Bombay where there are only three seasons — hot, very hot, and unbearably hot. It was a way to pass time between suburban train stations. Climbing off a local train onto the clamouring platform, holding the knitting needles aloft was always a good way to get those nimble-fingered and pinching rascals skipping neatly out of the way.

PERFECT PREFECT

SANGEETA VERMA

RECENTLY ADORNED WITH the title of 'Prefect' at school, my 16-year-old son promptly acquired the dictatorial traits of his forbears in this old Roman office. Puffing up with maternal pride at his elevation, I now looked forward to his being more responsible at home too. But I had another thing coming.

Reprimanded for an untidy room, he just listed his additional school duties. "Mum, I have to see that children attend morning assembly and not goof off in the back field or canteen." In short he was too pooped to do even his usual domestic chores. So the prefect's mother had to take on the additional burden of doing his bed and settling his cupboard, all in the greater cause of enabling the prefect to discharge his official duties more efficiently.

"I had to miss both periods of English because I was organizing the juniors for the school concert," he said one day soon after his anointment. If I detected a tinge of delight in his tone, I consciously dismissed the thought. "Today all through the history class I was involved in selecting the middle school team for a quiz contest," he announced another day. I was impressed but concerned. Weren't the responsibilities falling into a pattern? All the English and history classes were obviously dispensable.

I started to worry. How would he complete his course on his own? What will happen to his result? Maybe I started to nag just a wee bit. "Mum, you are just like Lenin. 'Study, study, study and study'. Is that all a student should do?" Keen to reassert my ideological leanings as the fun-loving, liberal mother I had always prided myself on being, I rapidly withdrew.

Unaware of the pattern at school, his father was very disturbed by the Internet addiction at home. He changed the password one day and barred the boy's access. My son promptly shaved off his head (to lament the demise of democracy in the home, he said) and started to grow a beard. To be shaved off when normalcy was restored, he stated. Within a month he was sporting a beard. His appearance acquired a venerable dimension making it impossible to reprimand him or to question his actions.

The only one unaffected by all this upheaval was my younger son. A self-assured pre-teen he had acquired the arsenal for survival against an elder sibling early in life. Thrilled at his brother's elevation but never in awe, he continued to challenge big brother at every turn. His tone and manner became increasingly authoritative. I concluded that this resulted from proximity to the powers that be. He was after all the prefect's younger brother.

Ever so gradually a new trend emerged. The younger one always seemed to be informing the elder one about school announcements. Puzzled, I expressed surprise at the prefect's consistent lack of information. My younger son patiently explained, "Mummy, *bhaiya* is never at the school assembly. He's always in the back field. Actually, he bunks to catch the bunkers." Obviously, authority flows from knowing the dark secrets of those in power.

BASIC INSTINCT

PV NARAYANA SWAMY

THE TOI OF December 26, 1999 had quoted William Mitchell to say, "The new digital order will not turn us all into rootless, lap-top toting, cell-phoning nomads. Most of us will still want more or less permanent places of our own".

The insatiable human craze for self-importance is nothing new. Even Lord Krishna's brother Balarama was overly fond of adulation. The wily and wicked Duryodhana capitalized on it by entertaining him with a lavish feast. Balarama, feeling deeply indebted, chose not to side with the Pandavas in the Kurukshetra war. He distanced himself from both the parties by going on a long pilgrimage.

Kalidasa was the greatest poet ever in Sanskrit. Yet Dhananjaya, an also-ran in the field, thought too highly of himself when he had the cheek to denigrate Kalidasa in a *sloka* meaning "Magha had committed a hundred grammatical errors, Bhasa three hundred, but Kalidasa with supercilious nonchalance changed *apa* in the *sloka* to *aapa* and gave back in the same coin."

In Sanskrit, *aapa* means water, and the changed meaning was: Magha used hundred synonyms for water, Bhasa three hundred, but Kalidasa innumerable. For Dhananjaya the only term was *aapa, aapa* and nothing else. It shows his limited vocabulary. What was aimed as a brickbat of criticism was turned into a bouquet of accolade. Coming to later times, about six decades back, C — a lady social worker in K-state — had the singular good fortune to go West as a leader of a committee. Feeling highly egoistic about her role, she wrote a book, *The Europe I Saw*. In it, every page was full of anecdotes in first person singular, and every photograph had an oft-repeated central figure — the authoress. The book was commented upon by a reviewer well known for calling a spade a spade, in one sentence: "The title of the book needs to be changed to *I ..... Who saw Europe.*"

A senior colleague was known among our group as 'the first person singular'. He would nauseatingly catalogue his abilities and achievements at the slightest pretext. Once during a party, he was in his usual element, saying one should taste evil to know and avoid it. He said he had smoked, taken drinks — actually he was in high spirits — tried drugs, etc at least once. He condescendingly confided, "No use being goody-goody in this world. You should indulge in every thing undesirable at least once."

Remembering what I had recently read in a book, I blurted out that "there is one thing you should not try even once". Pat came his reaction, "Tell me and I shall go for it."

I replied, "Suicide".

His discomfiture can be more imagined than penned. Human nature, it is said, is so complex as to bear comparison with a blind man looking in a dark room for a black cat which is not there. Indeed Dale Carnegie hit the nail on it's head, saying all human activities are traceable to one basic instinct, the desire to grow important in the eyes of others.

LIGHTNESS OF BEING

KRISHAN KALRA

IT WAS A muggy June evening. I had left Lucknow early enough to catch the night train from Kanpur. We made it to the Ganges bridge in good time but now, with hardly an hour to go, we were stuck in a traffic jam. I had waited for over 15 minutes in the car. Exasperated at the delay, I got down and started pacing up and down the sidewalk, mumbling to myself, swearing and cursing everything in sight.

Perhaps five minutes passed like this. Suddenly I heard someone from another car calling out to me, "Come here." The man beckoned with his hand too. An old man, perhaps 65, clad in dhoti and kurta, sprawled on the rear seat, one arm under his head, car doors open, he appeared surprisingly calm. I was still debating whether to respond when he called out again, "Didn't you hear me, young man. I'm calling you?"

I didn't like his tone. But I went up to him. The man took his time to speak again, pulled up his legs and motioned for me to sit. I thought he was very rude but something made me sit down uncomfortably next to this uncouth person, who was meddling in my affairs. "What's your problem, why are you so tense?" were his next words. I was ready to snub him and get up but something stopped me. "You must be mad at me," he seemed to read my thoughts. "That's the problem with young people. No patience, always worked up, always in a tearing hurry. Now, relax and tell me what's bothering you? Are you worried about missing a train?" I had actually calmed down. This simple man was making sense.

"As a matter of fact, I do want to catch a train. I had left Lucknow in good time, but now this stupid traffic." Lalaji interrupted me, "Here you go again. Now listen. First of all there is still a chance of your reaching the station on time. And even if you don't, heavens won't fall. You might miss some appointments, may be a board meeting. Whatever; I can assure you it would not be earth shattering, it won't even cause a national calamity. Your generation is unnecessarily worked up. You all feel that your shoulders carry the entire burden of the world. No such thing, my friend, you are only a cog in the wheel, a small cog indeed."

Surprisingly, I felt lighter. Missing the train won't really matter. I could ring up and explain to the client who was coming next morning. As I sat there, next to this shabbily-dressed, half-literate man, I saw the truth in his earthy advice. I realized the folly of fretting over events beyond control. I began to appreciate the wisdom of leaving certain things to take their own course. I silently thanked the meddling Lalaji.

PAKISTAN ZINDABAD

SHASTRI RAMACHANDARAN

"PAKISTAN WILL COLLAPSE", said our strategic seer. Ever since these words have been uttered, they have been the cause of recurrent nightmares. Not just because of the job of editing middles. Middles, as middle-writers, middle-editors and middle-readers know, thrive on Pakistan. Of course, we have the odd ones about cats and dogs, Delhi's buses and Mumbai's trains, biscuits and bakeries, Shabana Azmi and Amitabh Bachchan. But the staple of middles is Pakistan. From the conflicts of 1948, 1965 and 1971 and the nuclear tests in both countries, to the Lahore bus ride and Kargil the troubled history of the two is an unending reservoir of middle matter. When the men in uniform are on alert their wives write in heart-tugging pieces. And when the men in uniform are at leisure they love to do this chore themselves.

More than middles, which would lose their spark and fight, the editorial page would become insufferably dull without all those edits. Eleven out of 10 edits deal with Pakistan, Kargil, nuclear deterrence, India-Pakistan relations, foreign secretary-level talks, resuming or cancelling the buses and trains which connect the neighbours, and of course, the oppressive absence of democracy in that military dictatorship. How on earth would newspapers fill up the editorial columns and what would the edit writers do without a hostile Pakistan?

Not just the edit page, but the entire newspaper would face a drought of material but for the existence of Pakistan. Their dictatorship makes us feel good about our democracy. Their ex-prime minister in danger of being hanged makes us feel liberal about our own ex-PMs hanging around. As much as media, the entertainment world has been enriched. Had there been no Lahore, where would Bollywood villains KN Singh, Ajit and Pran have come from, leaving real-world villainy where it belongs; where would the bus have gone to with Atal Behari Vajpayee if there was no Lahore and in Pakistan? The world of films and arts had something to get worked up about, thanks to Kargil releasing their creative juices and patriotic fervour.

India would never have had anything remotely approximating 'art in the time of war' but for Kargil. Beyond media and arts, the government itself would find itself at a loose, and losing, end without Pakistan. Good boy George at the defence ministry is convinced that had it not been for the Kargil conflict, the defence budget would be less than our outlays for health and education. And dashing-about-the-world Jaswant Singh would have been left speechless in NAM and other places but for Pakistan being not only a dictatorship but also a "terrorist state".

Pakistan has given India a cause both at home and abroad. At home it is the familiar enemy and abroad we are building awareness of why and how Pakistan must be isolated. Should Pakistan collapse, we would feel worthless, become workless and be deprived of a basis for patriotism. If Pakistan didn't exist, we would have had to invent it.

TAILOR-MADE SOLDIER

ANIL B SAWANT

ON THE TV when I saw our jawans fire heavy artillery at the enemy-occupied cliffs of Kargil, my mind raced back to a nondescript shop in my native town, Ratnagiri. It belonged to Dhondoo Tailor. His passion was the newspaper. The whole morning he would read the national or foreign news and brood over a specific topic in the afternoon. By evening his analyses would be ready.

During my college days, I once went to him to get my naval NCC uniform altered. This otherwise quiet man suddenly came alive and spoke knowledgeably about ranks and weapons, revealing a deep interest in military matters. Since I was aspiring to join the Navy, an everlasting bond developed between us.

In 1962, as the clouds of war loomed over our border with China, Dhondoo became restless. Out of his meagre savings, he bought a radio. Now his day was wholly devoted to newspapers and radio. He pinned a map of the North East Frontier Agency (NEFA) in his shop. Thangla Ridge, Sela Pass, Dhola, Bomdilla, the airfields at Leh and Chusul, the monastery town of Tawang and Namka Chu river were neatly highlighted. News from the battlefront would be analyzed after referring to the map. As the border skirmishes resulted in war, Dhondoo was a man possessed. Often he would launch scathing attacks on the Chinese leaders. Our political leadership also was not spared. Stories of valour and grit displayed by our ill-equipped jawans would moisten his eyes.

Since the war ended as a military debacle, a severely depressed Dhondoo would not talk to anyone for days. The shine in his eyes was now missing, his voice was faint and handshake feeble. Looking blank, he said after a long pause, "Do you know why it happened? The enemy had built roads to hasten their supplies. Our supplies were slow because mules had to haul loads on steep inclines." He demonstrated with his palms how Indian soldiers were trapped on the lower slopes while the Chinese were at a much higher altitude. He said, "It was easy for them to target us. That's why we found the going tough". At 16, I was impressed by this strategic analysis.

When I joined the Navy, Dhondoo Tailor was overjoyed. During visits to Ratnagiri, I would often be there at his shop — mostly listening. Then came the 1971 war and Pakistan's surrender at Dhaka. During my next visit, I proudly went to see Dhondoo, to show him my newly-earned Poorvi Star and Sangram Medal. A map of erstwhile East Pakistan hung there with Comilla, Chittagong, Jessore, Khulna and Dhaka neatly highlighted. With a forlorn look, his son informed me that when news of the Pakistani surrender came over the radio, an emotionally-charged Dhondoo had burst crackers, hugged passers-by and distributed sweets. For him it was a mission accomplished, a time to celebrate. But, the celebrations were shortlived. Next morning Dhondoo died. I kept gazing at his photograph, hung my medals on both sides of it and saluted Dhondoo — a tailor by profession but a soldier at heart.

DIFFERENT STROKES

MUKUND B KUNTE

DAWN FRASER, WHO along with her brother had splashed a lot of history in Olympic swimming pools, has recently been honoured with a 'Champion of the Century' award in Vienna. In the December of 1964, she was on the Frontier Mail on which I was returning to Bombay after the Services Tennis championships in Delhi.

On the Indian Railways, then, one could order a meal either in your compartment or go to the dining car. My wife and I took the latter option for lunch. On that famous train those days, before the Rajdhani and other superfast expresses overtook her, they served you comfortably seated at well laid out tables. Unlike the present, one could safely leave the luggage behind, and so at Sawai Madhaopur we found ourselves at a table for four. Our companions turned out to be two astounding swimmers of the time, the Australians Dawn Fraser and Linda Mcgill. Fate must have willed it and the meal became memorable because people from Down Under, 'diggers' as the Brits used to call them, are such friendly travellers and, over lunch, conversation flowed like wine. At Ratlam we returned to our bogies after exchanging addresses.

Linda and Dawn were taking the land and sea route to England after the Tokyo Olympics. Sensational performers of the time, they had been in the news not just for the gold medals they had won but also for their 'close-fisted' protest salutation at the march past of the Games. They were sight-seeing in India and, taking up our offer of hospitality, dropped in at our Queen's Road flat. We took them to my ship INS Brahmaputra. In our ship's Ward Room they were an instant success, the bachelors taking over with alacrity from then on; and not surprisingly, the girls were seen the next day riding pillion on the scooters of two gallant shipmates.

In November last, Dawn — winner of gold medals in three successive Olympics — hit the headlines in the company of the Brazilian soccer idol Pele and two Americans, the boxer Mohammed Ali and swimmer Mark Spitz. They were honoured as the 'Top Ten' sports personalities of the 20th century, by an international jury headed by Juan Antonio Samaranch. She told the audience in the packed State Opera House in Vienna, that, coming from a working class family, she couldn't afford to take up her favourite sport, horse riding; whereas all she needed for swimming was a suit and a towel.

That December, Linda Mcgill, incidentally, was on her way to the UK to swim the English Channel and Dawn was her manager. Linda had confided to us that doubtless she would cross the channel but she would improve the timing, clipping many minutes, by doing it in the nude. We later read a Fleet Street story flashed by the British press that Britain would have none of it — not without the swimsuit.

POLL ROLL PUZZLE

MN CHATTERJEE

IT WAS A curious experience. While I was dutifully exercised about my right to vote, the local election machinery thought otherwise; it seemed hell-bent on keeping the ballot paper out of my reach. In the process, I was initiated into the mysteries of a new technique, showing how deftly the tail could wag the dog in the crucible of democracy.

It all began in May '99, amidst the media hype surrounding the special awareness drive, launched on the lines of the pulse polio campaign, to register voters for the ensuing Lok Sabha and assembly elections in Maharashtra. After making enquiries, I sought out the office of the local *tehsildar*, where the *naib-tehsildar* was overseeing the entire electoral operation. I asked to see the latter and was directed to a table in the remote corner of a decrepit hall and found myself talking to a face partly hidden by papers stacked on the table.

"After my retirement in Mumbai, I have shifted to Kalyan. I would like to get my name and my wife's included in the local electoral rolls. May I have the application forms, please?"

"You may not", was the terse reply. "The dealing assistant is out. You will have to wait".

"But are these not the relevant forms?" I asked, pointing to the stacks on his table. But he clammed up, even when I queried whether he was indeed the person I had asked to see. He was sitting idle. Since I was staying a bit far I preferred to hang around outside, instead of going back. I got two sets of printed forms against my receipt, after an hour-long wait. A week later, I was back again with the 50-odd columns in both the forms duly filled, along with photocopies of the ration card. But the forms were not accepted, because the separate cell set up for the purpose functioned from 10am to 1pm and it was already 1.30pm.

Next day, I reached there at 10.30am, only to find the door closed. The neighbouring stamp-vendor, to whom I must have become a familiar face by now, offered me a stool to rest.

Mercifully, the door opened soon, to a poky little room. After a close scrutiny and some questioning, the forms were accepted, to my great relief. A receipt was issued with some initials scribbled on it and the space marked for the 'Seal of ERO' left blank. Both the names were wrongly spelt though they had been written in capitals in the forms.

A month later, my wife spoke of a waspish visitor who introduced himself as a government worthy engaged in electoral work. He made some routine queries and left. However, when the voters' lists were put up towards the end of July, I was amazed to see that our names had been included only to be cut out later in ink. None of the electoral staff could explain the mystery.

DIFFERENT STROKES

MURAD ALI BAIG

IN OCTOBER 2002, I was at Suzuka, Japan. While waiting for the Formula 1 race to start I asked my friend Akitoshi, who is involved with Toyota projects in Asia, how Toyota found Indian workers as compared to other Asian workers. He did not reply and I thought he had not heard my question. Then he suddenly said, "Chopsticks". I was confused so he elaborated, "Indian people eat with their hands. Make a mess everywhere. They do not know about accuracy and precision."

Though I tried to explain that eating with fingers required a special etiquette, I began to understand what he meant. I'm not sure that chopsticks is the complete explanation but Indians do tend to spread things about and do things in a messy and chaotic way unlike their less imaginative but more precise East Asian counterparts. On the other hand this seemingly haphazard way, like India's chaotic traffic, makes Indians great with innovative abstractions.

Most Indians are great thinkers and talkers and when faced with any difficulty they can quickly visualize numerous possible solutions and immediately pronounce the predictable words, "No problem." By contrast, their chopstick wielding counterparts are usually slow to take a decision until every possibility has been thoroughly examined. Then, they move fast with the best solution.

Worldwide, Toyota does not encourage individual brilliance but has demonstrated brilliant results from group effort where many ordinary people are motivated to extraordinary performance.

To manage their Indian shop-floor workers, Toyota carefully studies the quality of potential workers rather than their qualifications. Matriculation is essential for filling in reports and punching key boards but it is both the minimum as well as the maximum qualification required. There are exhaustive tests to evaluate character, personality, physique, energy and attitudes So a worker is taught to do exactly what he has to do and is not encouraged to think. Especially as careless thinking often leads to disturbing well-established systems. They are not taught how to use chop sticks but this training in precision is perhaps the secret of Toyota's fabled product quality.

Akitoshi then disrupted my train of thought by saying, "Indian engineers and managers — very good." A view shared by many foreign companies operating in India. One FMCG company manager once said to me, "If we could find a country with Indian managers and Chinese workers we would become world beaters." Are chopsticks the answer?

STICKY WICKET

SK DEV VERMAN

I AM NOT much of a cricket fan or follower. But my knowledge of the game goes a little deeper than my interest in it. That, I suppose, is inevitable in a country where cricket can influence election campaigns, alternately put the nation in a 'feel bad' mode and, as I learnt recently, freeze marital relations.

My family largely shares my lack of enthusiasm for India's national game. My daughter is of an age where she finds Barbie and doll-houses more interesting and my son prefers soccer. My wife's interest in the game matches that of my children.

Dark clouds however appeared on the horizon recently. The wife and I were surfing channels one evening when we chanced upon the live telecast of the third one-dayer between Pakistan and India.

She queried, "Weren't they showing this a few days ago?"

"This is the third one-dayer," I explained.

"You mean this is the third day they are playing?" she enquired.

"Yes and no. This is the third day they are playing but it is the third match of the series which consists of matches played only for one-day each," I pointed out.

The wife persisted, "If it's a one-day match why are they still playing on the third day?"

"It's not the same match. This is match number three, different from match number one and two, which have already been played on two other days before this, which is why this is the third day," I explained patiently.

"Oh," said she. The tone and tenor of the "oh" suggested that the debate wasn't over yet. "Who is winning?" she demanded to know.

"No one," I replied. "You mean it's a draw?" she asked.

"Yes and no. The match is still on and therefore both teams have a chance. Who wins will depend on which team scores more runs at the end of the day," I explained again.

"You mean no team has scored so far?" she asked again.

Before I could tell the score she interrupted, "How many goals has Pakistan scored?"

I took a deep breath and prepared to conclude the debate without further ado. "One does not score goals in cricket. Runs are scored and wickets taken in order to win. You score runs by running and take wickets by, well, by taking wickets, if you know what I mean. Nothing could be simpler."

The wife said, "Oh" again in a tone that seemed to suggest that she thought that I was not being entirely honest with her and this was something that was expected from me anyway.

BEST FOOT FORWARD

V SAPATNEKAR

IT WAS DECEMBER 1992, when events at Ayodhya had boiled over. Earlier, our Army unit had been ordered to have a 'flying column' ready in aid of civil authority — represented in this case by a young District Magistrate. An affable and entirely likable gentleman with a fine reputation for competence and impartiality.

That night the 'flying column' was called out to restore law and order in a nearby downtown area where riots had broken out. Acting with alacrity, the column sped through a maze of dark, crooked streets leading off into narrow lanes with rows of dark houses lined on either side. As the column marched down one such street, it came under a fusillade of bricks, stones, rotten vegetables and even volleys from country-made pistols and muzzle loaders. The column quickly fanned out and systematically began house and street clearing drills.

Slowly order was restored and quite a few 'anti-social' elements were rounded up. During this rounding up, a huddled figure suddenly darted from a darkened doorway, flung a petrol bomb at the leading jeep and melted into the shadows. The spare cans of petrol in the jeep immediately went up in fire. By its light we saw that the arsonist had scaled a nearby wall and escaped into an old *haveli* surrounded by a fruit orchard. The troops quickly cordoned off the *haveli* and the DM and the police were called to smoothen out the legalities for a house search.

The *haveli* was a vast structure with some dozen rooms furnished in a manner which left no doubt about the purpose for which they were used. Each room was thoroughly searched, but except for an ancient crone who could hardly move, there appeared to be no one around. As the search was about to be called off, there came the faint tinkle of bangles. Closer scrutiny revealed a secret passage behind a cupboard. But before it could be forced, the old woman set up such a shindig about trespassing, the modesty of her 'ladies' and the late hour that the DM called a truce till day-break.

Next morning nine women emerged from the secret passage. But they were so heavily veiled that it was impossible to ascertain whether the bomb thrower was disguised as one of them. The police had no women constables on duty to do a more intimate search. Finally the good DM intervened and whispered something in the old woman's ear. She nodded and then conducted her 'ladies' into an open garden and across a shallow water channel. As they traipsed across the water one by one, the women raised their voluminous skirts above their ankles to prevent them from getting wet. The DM looked on; his eyes lowered to the ground in a show of decorum.

As soon as the women had crossed over, he suddenly laid his hand on one of them. There was instant bedlam. But amongst the babble there was also a swear in an unmistakably manly voice. At last we had our man — all because he failed to put his best foot forward.

GIFT OF GIVING

GEORGE MENEZES

THIS IS OUR story. The old girl's and mine. Who knows, one day it may also be your story. In our years on the planet we have been privileged to have many generous friends. Some of them have taught us that you don't need an occasion for gift-giving. We have been blessed not by the quantity of their giving but by the quality of their generosity.

There is something magical about gifts. It transforms both the giver and the recipient. If the gift is given with only ribbons and no strings attached. If the gift is given for no reason at all. Just for the joy of giving. If it is given not merely out of plenty but out of material poverty and the richness of someone's heart.

More than the giver, blessed are those who receive with a spirit of joy, eyes glowing, mouth wide open like a child at a birthday party. All giving and all gifts are priceless, as we discovered after we were told in the antiseptic room of a warm and loving doctor that the old girl was heading for irreversible and total kidney failure.

In the failing of her kidney I faulted the Lord. Forgetting the million times I, her husband, for 40 years had failed her. She, on the other hand, totally surrendered herself to the Almighty and carried on as if nothing had happened. And so we took on a hectic schedule of travelling to places she had always wanted to go. We travelled to Mauritius and China. We enjoyed a laid-back, chauffeur-driven journey along the Garden Route from Port Elizabeth to Cape Town in South Africa. But we could not beat the dialysis-clock forever. When the time came and we started to experience the imprisonment of it all, I wrote to the old girl's siblings to ask for the gift of a kidney. When her brother Cyril wrote, "You can have my kidney. If I had two hearts I would have given you one," the journey of faith for us, for our relatives, friends and neighbours had just begun.

Three months after a successful kidney transplant the kidney developed a cancerous growth caused by the anti-rejection drug. It was a "one in a million case," they said. Our friends and our doctor's friends from the USA arranged the intervention of Harvard Medical School who advised an expensive line of treatment and the withdrawal of the anti-rejection drug. To kill the life-threatening cancer it was necessary to allow the kidney to be rejected and go back to dialysis.

"No way," said the old girl, "it is my own brother's kidney. He gave it to me from the abundance of his love. God will not allow a gift of love to be rejected."

"Bravo," said our doctor, always ready to take up a new challenge. We went dancing the other night defying death and dialysis. We visited our daughter in England and friends in Germany. If you are giving gifts, we told them, why not gift a kidney?

MAID OF HONOUR

RENUKA VISHWANATHAN

IT IS MORNING and as I fumble my way to the kitchen, I step warily, fearful of making any noise lest I wake her up before time. That would be catastrophic. Her tea is made and she takes it immediately on getting up. I thank my stars that she doesn't expect bed tea.

I finish my morning chores and ask her to make what she wants for lunch. "I don't like brinjals," she says, annoyed by what she sees on peering into the refrigerator. I apologize and promise to stock up other vegetables which she likes. I leave for office, and get involved in my day's work. I ring up exactly at 1pm as I know that after this hour she has her afternoon nap and does not like to be disturbed.

"Is everything alright?" I ask her apologetically.

"Of course," she snaps back. And as an after-thought, "Don't come late. My whole routine gets upset."

I nod silently into the phone. I make my way home in the evening rush hour. I am not late. The days I am late, I am met with sniffs and sulks and the evenings are ruined. I sit with the children and help them with their homework. She has to eat dinner by 9pm. Food is kept in the warmer for my husband, and we all gulp down our dinner, before her time.

Work is over and she relaxes, watching television with us. Bed time is at 10pm for her come hell or high water.

"You really spoil her," my husband grumbles. "You treat her

much better than you treat me," he cribs.

Our annual vacations are planned around her. My leave record depends upon her. Without her, I cannot manage even one day of my career. She is a blessing and God's own gift to women like me. It is essential to keep her in good humour as the house will run smoothly and the children be well looked after. Annoy her and we are subjected to burnt food, sloppy house work, neglected children and threats of leaving.

Yes, she is my maid and my major support. I wake up every day in dread that she will say she wants to go. For there is always the threat of her being enticed with a higher salary by unscrupulous neighbours. I regularly appease her with new and old clothes and gifts. After all, my going to work depends on her, and she is essential. Like my husband would say, "I am expendable, but she is not." And that sums it all up.

A HOAX CALL

SUREKHA MOHAN

THE LAND OF the black gold beckoned the couple and the call was too tempting to resist. He was a banker and had secured a plum job in one of the Gulf countries. She was a teacher and was assured of good prospects there. So they and their nine-year-old daughter bade goodbye to their friends and relations back home in their coastal town and flew out with stars in their eyes.

Things worked out as planned. The couple began minting money. As luck would have it, their neighbour happened to be from their home state. What is more the lady of the house was a teacher, too, while her husband worked in a Gulf airline. They, too, had a daughter about 10 years old. The two families became good friends. The girls would come home together from school and stay together waiting for their parents to return. The idiot box made a cozy three-some.

Life could not have been any better away from home — good money, good employers and Indian friends to boot. A year went by and though home-sick, the moolah kept them going. But then a phone-call shattered their fragile haven. That day, the two couples had left for their respective offices as usual. In the afternoon, they had rung up home to inquire about their children's welfare on their return from school. Everything was normal. Then, after a couple of hours, out of the blue, urgent summons forced them to rush home from office. The place was swarming with cops and their two little darlings, teary-eyed and frightened, were waiting for them. Somebody had rung up the airlines office where the father of one of the girls worked and warned that a bomb was planted in a plane. This led to a scare and a thorough check of the plane before the call was found out to be a hoax. When the call came the second time, the authorities were ready and it was promptly traced. After that the game was up and unmasking the prankster was not really difficult.

To everyone's surprise it turned out that the two little girls were the culprits. The overdose of television had taken its toll. With time hanging on their hands, the little imps took inspiration from one of the serials they had watched on the idiot box to conjure up the prank, hardly realizing its grave consequences.

For the parents, it was curtains. They were given just a day's time to quit the country or face action against the girls. Their dream-run shattered by the precocious little imps, the two families had no option but to end their Gulf odyssey and return home to build their life again from scratch. It was a snakes and ladders game all over again.

RITES OF PASSAGE

JB D'SOUZA

INTIMATIONS OF MORTALITY come quite early in life. To me the first of them came on one of the numerous transfers my political bosses found necessary. Each time one is transferred one's juniors in the office feel obliged to hold a farewell ceremony, with speeches extolling the departing soul's qualities. On one occasion I was stunned when a speaker said he had risen to pay me his "last respects". I didn't know what to make of that; but the next speech was less comforting than baffling. "Many Happy Returns," the speaker wished me. At my age now, there are fewer and fewer friends still surviving. When I meet one of them, it is generally at a funeral, and the usual question is why I was not at Peter's funeral. Or Raman's, or someone else's. Funerals are highlights in old people's lives.

They are sombre special occasions, the only ones where senior citizens can meet. *The Times* obit columns record the latest passages to a heavenly abode. Each morning I scan those columns to learn of yesterday's departures. The yellow pages of Mumbai's telephone directory list many options for this transition to heaven. The entries are understandably terse, but if you call up you will discover at least one "Undertaker bespoke, by appointment to His Excellency the governor's" (whatever those words mean). An operator who promises travel in a really luxurious hearse. At the pearly gates, St Peter will be powerfully impressed.

For lesser fry, there are lesser options. Undertaker Michael Pinto tempts you with hospitality. His invitation, in giant letters, "When you drop dead, drop in," adorns the facade of his Lady Jamsetjee Road headquarters, on one of Mumbai's main streets. It has evidently succeeded; more clients dropped in than Pinto expected. He has had to expand into a much larger place down the road, and to open branches elsewhere. Undertakers can be quite versatile and hi-tech in the passages they advertise. They not only offer to burn or bury you. They are ready to pack you off to distant lands of your choice, maybe even to your heavenly abode. "Body sent by air, rail, road, fax," reads Edward Jones' entry in the yellow pages. None of his competitors match that. They can be ingenious too. At one funeral some years ago, the corpse lay at the graveside amid a group of mourners, while the undertaker led them in a prayer. Suddenly a piercing shriek stopped the ceremonies. "I saw his eyes flutter, his hands move," screamed the dead man's daughter. No one knew what to do.

The funeral director asked if there was a doctor present to examine the body. No one came forward. Twilight was already failing. With a flash of inspiration our resourceful funeral director, clearly an ardent democrat, decided on a vote. He asked how many mourners thought the man was dead. "Those in favour?" The response was positive. The ayes had it; the man was declared truly dead, and was duly buried. The rites decorously completed, the undertaker raced off, to measure his next client.

ALPHABET SOUP

SANDY SUNDARAM

IN THE WONDERFUL 1930s, our school believed in making us good all-round citizens. It was bent on making us worldly-wise, to get into the best companies and be good Box-wallahs. There was a belief that General Knowledge (GK) was important and so, every week, a quiz was conducted about events around the globe.

It was not the era of acronyms and abbreviations and there were few if any, but our masters wanted us to be well versed in AD, BC, USA, USSR and the learnable lot. We boys crammed all that and more. Whether R — got in because of his GK or his boxing, another R — for his cricket, or L — because he was a Rhodes Scholar, can now be only relegated to the realm of conjecture. But they all rose to great heights.

Came World War II and abbreviations and acronyms multiplied faster than the proverbial rabbits. The few who came to our school from England and the better known schools brought a wealth of War-generated slang and song; the former enlarging our savvy more than all the acronyms. The proliferation of radio stations all over the world opened up new juxtapositions in alphabets and numbers like WGEO and KG210. This probably laid the foundation for the future 'HAM' in me.

University and the engineering college opened the flood-gates of technical jargon and the peace of 1945 gave birth to a plethora of acronyms with the UN agencies taking the lion's share. In retrospect, I am glad that the Central Services examinations were held in abeyance because, seeing the kind of GK questions that have been set, I doubt if I could have crammed all those alphabetical nightmares and become a Collector or an IG or a Director-General of whatever.

I knew what AIR meant and joined, learning new acronyms. But I left it at the earliest to join another set of alphabets —IMA. The Army, I said to myself, is bound to have very little of that nonsense of an alphabetic soup. Alas for innocence; one had to run pretty fast to be with evolving technology and to keep up with the new oral shorthand. C21 became C31 to transform into C312 and is still growing; S+DX, D70, WS19HP and many more with suffixes of MkII, MkIII etc.

For my sins, I got pitchforked into the computers division, which must get the palm — starting from IBM, OS, Kb, Mb, WP to Y2K and now ISP, and ye Gods what else.

To compound my misery, visiting a relation, I heard voices raised. YBF, cried the lady, to be followed by FEL and later by MIK. Ever seeker of things esoteric, I found that besides the commonly used CP, GK-I and GK-II, my hosts also freely used acronyms to say, 'You Bloody Fool', 'Family Eat Less' and 'More in the Kitchen'. OLIARFYOP (Oh Lord, I am ready for your presence) SAMEFA (Save me from Acronyms).

ROLL OF HONOUR

RAVI BATRA

THE LAST NIZAM of Hyderabad was an enormously rich man with a fabulous collection of jewellery. He owned many palaces, he was also a frugal person of simple habits. Dislodged from his power in the 'police action' of 1948, he spent the rest of his life in virtual seclusion. It is, therefore, extremely unlikely that he would have heard of, let alone lent his title to, the Nizam Restaurant which provided Calcutta with one of the jewels in its gastronomical crown — the famous kathi kebab roll.

Though the sun had set on the British Empire in 1947, it was still twilight ten years later, when I took up my first job in Calcutta. A number of British expatriates continued to be employed by mercantile firms. Bow ties and dinner jackets — black in winter and white in summer — were the men's formal evening wear. After a cocktail party, many Indian invitees would head for a late night movie. Nizam's, as it was popularly known, was located in close proximity to at least five cinema halls on, or slightly off, Chowringhee Street. It was convenient, as well as considered 'cool', to pick up a hot kathi roll as a substitute for dinner before the movie.

Bade Mian ruled his little empire with an iron ladle. He would first pour his special *maida* mix onto a heated iron plate to form the base for a circular paratha. "One or two eggs?" Bade Mian would ask. He would then drop the raw egg(s) into the paratha's centre. The convex side of the ladle was used to spread the egg evenly over the paratha which was flipped over twice so as to remain sunny side up. After it had turned a lovely golden-brown, he would ask, "One or two seekhs of kababs?"

The kababs had earlier been marinated in Bade Mian's secret masala tenderiser and were now barbecued over a coal fire. A small table fan kept the embers going and also carried the aroma of the kababs to Bade Mian, so that he would know when exactly they were ready. Finally, Bade Mian would add chopped onions and green chillies, a pinch of salt and the squeeze of a lemon. The paratha was then tightly rolled, wrapped in a newspaper and handed over in exchange for the princely sum of three rupees.

The newspaper served three purposes. First, it provided a convenient grip on the kathi roll. Second, it kept it warm, useful if there was still time for the movie. One could then drive down to the promenade along the Hooghly and eat it in a leisurely manner. Third, it sealed one end of the roll which prevented an errant kabab from slipping out and messing up one's dinner jacket. It wasn't just any old newspaper that was used. At that time there were only two venerable English language newspapers of Calcutta. So Bade Mian's third and final question before he wrapped the roll used to be, *"The Statesman* or the *Amrita Bazar Patrika?"*

THE SAIGAL SAGA

ASEEM K JHA

THE ENCHANTING NUMBER from *Street Singer*, *Babul mora naiher chhuto jai* came resonating from a road side tea-stall while I was going to fetch milk that morning. It acted as a soothing balm to the muse in me which has been somewhat debased by the hurly-burly of MTV, B4U and the like. I had to literally lend my ears to that icon of Hindi Cinema, Kundan Lal Saigal. I spontaneously looked at my wrist-watch. Yes, it was 7.55am. And it was KL Saigal indeed, signing off the morning show *Purani filmon ke geet* on Sri Lanka Broadcasting Corporation (SLBC).

It is SLBC that has kept alive the spirit of Saigal in the era of domineering satellite channels. It ends the morning half hour programme of old Hindi film songs, ritually, with a Saigal number. I still remember my father exhorting me, without looking at any watch, to hurry up for school even as Saigal's mellifluous voice emanating from the table-sized radiogram reverberated in our house. And the clock would strike eight in no time.

Those days we lived in a government quarter. Even at the fag end of his service, father had not been able to own or build a house. My mother was always carping at him for this 'remissness' on his part. To avoid nagging on this count, father would, at once, start singing *Ek bangla baney nyara...* the moment mother tried to raise the perennial issue. To this overture, she had no option but to give a gratifying smile. Being my father's son, I too follow the same escape route to evade my wife's pestering on sundry issues.

Whenever she sulks, and she does that quite often a la Mamatadi, I propitiate her not by conceding to her demands but simply by crooning that romantic number from the 1944 classic, *Meri Behan*, *Do naina matware tihare* or *Humse chhupo na o pyari sajaniya.* She is instantaneously placated and all smiles.

They say that Saigal was a woebegone singer of the blues. But it would be wrong to brand him thus. His audience was heterogeneous. *Jab dil hi toot gaya* became synonymous with the melancholy of broken hearts. *Chaah barbad karegi* echoed the Buddhist doctrine that desire is the root cause of human suffering. Of all the filmi lullabies that I hum to my little daughter Rangoli, it is still that evergreen number, *Soja raajkumari, soja* from the 1935 classic *Zindagi* that lulls her to slumber most comfortably. And she giggles her appreciation of my rendition, with a deliberate nasal accent, of the song-story *Ek raaje ka beta lekar* with equal fascination. This vindicates not only the versatility of Saigal, but also explains why he became a household name during the infancy of Bollywood in the 1930s and 1940s.

The transformation of this lanky lad of Jammu from a seller of Remington typewriters to a player of Dwarkin's harmonium is an absorbing story. And so is the nostalgia of those who lived in that blissful era of Indian film-music.

LITTLE INDIA INC

VIKRANT MAHAJAN

ASK ANY EXPATRIATE Indian living in the US about the most famous desi address there and pat comes the reply: Jackson Heights. Located in the Queens borough of New York City, this ethnic suburb is the Mecca for all Indian-Americans. Barely 20 minutes from midtown Manhattan by subway train, Jackson Heights provides the best acclimatization for any Indian who's just arrived in the Big Apple. The sights, sounds and smells here are all unmistakably Indian and right from the *aloo tikki* vendor to the roadside *paan wallah* to the haberdasher selling kurta pyjamas, one can flavour the best of India in this 'desi Times Square'.

One thing that Indians most miss abroad is the informal bazar that they've presumably left behind. It is here that Jackson Heights — or 'Jaikishan Heights', as it is jokingly called — comes to their rescue. A trip to this 'Little India' can whet any NRI's nostalgia for India almost instantly. Those yearning for Indian cuisine can find sheer bliss in *dhabas* like Mallika and Sher-e-Punjab. Jackson Diner is another widely-acclaimed restaurant where one can partake a buffet lunch featuring *murgh pasanda, tandoori naan, saag and besan halwa* for under 10 dollars (cheap by New York standards). A weekly visit to Jackson Heights is mandatory for many Indians living in the New York-New Jersey-Connecticut area for stocking up their domestic provisions. Grocery stores like Patel Supermarket and Apna Bazar overflow with spices and provisions imported straight from India. The *mithai* shops display mouthwatering delicacies like *burfis, jalebis* and *gulab jamuns* in attractive cases. Windows at jewellery stores like Gita and Queens beckon shoppers with exquisite 22-carat *jhumkas* and anklets.

74th Street in Jackson Heights, where the Indian presence is especially large and which is also one of the busiest subway stations in New York City, is dotted generously with salwar kameez boutiques. These are the favourite haunts for Indian trousseau shopping. Jackson Heights even has sprawling beauty parlours offering *mehndi* decorations. Bollywood hits waft out of Indian music shops where one can get CDs and videos of the latest Hindi films. Jackson Heights has a plethora of immigration lawyers, marriage bureaus and travel agencies specializing in tours to exotic Indian destinations. Those looking for an apartment rental among fellow Indians also find in Jackson Heights the best place to network. Tickets for Bollywood nites held frequently in neighbouring Long Island area can also be found with shopkeepers in Little India. The area resembles a crowded Indian marketplace, right down to its characteristic noise, and to many foreigners, it means the next best thing to visiting India. Not only Indians but Pakistanis and Bangladeshis, too, find this suburb a comforting nest, where they can meet their own kind. Jackson Heights is truly a cornucopia of desi experiences, promising one a home away from home. After spending interminable hours, one reluctantly leaves this place with the feeling, *ab India door nahin.*

BOLSHIE BRAHMIN

PM WARRIER

IN THE MID-'30s we often had total strangers for Kerala. My eldest brother, an unemployed graduate, had become the 1 secretary of the newly formed 'Young Men's Association and Club' of our village. Although non-political, the club used to invite leaders of the national movement for lectures. Thanks to my brother, the leaders often landed at our place.

Ours was a large joint family in those days, presided over by my grandmother, then in her early 60s. My brother was the eldest resident male member of the family. Grandmother learned through the grapevine that my brother's guests were often men of lower castes who would normally not be entertained in the house. She did not like it a bit but she chose to hold her peace.

One day a dark young man in a dhoti and a half-sleeved shirt (both *khadi*) appeared at our door and was received warmly by my brother. After an exchange of pleasantries, my brother sent word to our cook, Rama Warrier, to fetch a glass of buttermilk for the visitor. Rama Warrier nearly swooned at the sight of the visitor, for he was a Namboodiri from his village. The visitor greeted him genially but Rama Warrier seemed troubled. He had never served food or drink to a Brahmin. It was sinful for a Warrier, a non-Brahmin, to do so.

Word soon spread through the household about the strange Namboodiri who had no qualms about drinking buttermilk from a Warrier household. The womenfolk of the household were shocked. There were whispered speculations of how grandmother would take it. Grandmother, who was in bed with a touch of flu, was pained. It was no sin entertaining a member of a lower caste, but feeding a Brahmin was a different matter altogether. It could bring ghastly retributions on the family. As she lay there agonizing over my brother's indiscretion, one of the children excitedly reported to her that the visitor was having lunch. The news shattered her. She closed her eyes and started chanting the name of the Lord. The visitor departed in the evening. Grandmother's fever shot up that night and she became delirious. Everyone blamed it on my brother, who took it philosophically.

Fear of an impending doom seized us, the smaller children of the family. It was then that Rama Warrier offered a ray of hope. Someone asked him whether he didn't fear any retribution for having served lunch to a Brahmin. He remained thoughtful for a moment. This Namboodiri, he then told us, although from a noble family, was not a good Brahmin. He had entered politics, joined the Congress and mixed with all sorts of low-caste men, and was therefore a fallen Brahmin. No sin could accrue by feeding such a man, he said. He lowered his voice and added that it was even said he had become a Communist and that he would some day end up in jail. "They don't even refer to him as a Namboodiri any more," he said. "They call him Eeyemmess!"

It wasn't until years later that we learned Rama Warrier was an ardent admirer of EMS Namboodiripad. By then, of course, most of us were!

THE BEACHCOMBER

RAJ CHATTERJEE

THIS WAS DURING World War II. I was stationed at Bombay. Portuguese Goa was a favourite touring area for me and my colleagues. Scotch whisky had gone up to Rs16 per bottle in the metropolis and it was always possible to smuggle in a bottle or two from Goa where it cost Rs6. On one such visit to Panjim in 1942, I parked myself at the Casino Mira-Mer on the beach. Despite its name, it did not boast of a gaming table. An open-sided hall served as the receptionist's office, bar, dining room and lounge. The living accommodation consisted of sparingly furnished but clean huts.

I observed a figure stretched on a long, cane chair in the lounge. In his late sixties, dressed in a multi-coloured sarong and a white vest, the man didn't look very tall and had a slight paunch. The sparse hair on his head was snow-white and he wore a pince-nez over which he glanced at me for a second and then went back to the newspaper in his hands. Apart from me, he seemed to be the only guest at the Casino.

After dinner, over a bottle of cognac that cost me Rs5, we got talking. He was a Welshman who had spent most of his working life in the Federated Malay States doing a variety of jobs like that of an accountant to a rubber estate, club secretary, librarian and hotel manager. From the way he spoke I wasn't surprised to learn that he had been to a good public school in England and Oxford. He now subsisted on a small private income from investments in the UK. As we parted, I asked him if he could lend me something to read. He led me to his shack, went inside and brought out a book the title of which I was unable to read in the dark. Back in my quarters, I saw that he had given me a copy of Tennyson's poems — not quite my cup of tea. On the fly-leaf, in fading ink, there was his name and the inscription, 'Merton College, Oxford, Oct 1899'. A few months later, I ran into my Casino acquaintance at the India Coffee House in Bombay. His hair was neatly trimmed. He wore a well-pressed tussore suit and brown, suede shoes. We sat down at the same table and he offered me his case which held imported cigarettes, then obtainable only at black market prices.

He told me that he was helping a UK firm of publishers who were short of staff for the duration. He was staying at a boarding house in Colaba where he would be happy to entertain me. Somehow, I never got round to visit him and, a year later, my conscience smote me when I read of his death in the TOI. The notice had been put in by his landlady who wanted to know if anyone could give her his home address so that she could forward his personal belongings to his next of kin. I doubted if she ever got a reply. Also, I wondered if he had any 'next of kin' or if his belongings amounted to much more than a battered silver cigarette case and a calf-bound volume of Tennyson.

BOON OF A TOWN

NANDINI SEN GUPTA

I HAVE ALWAYS been a tad conscious of my antecedents. You see, I am a townie. Meaning, I grew up in a small company township called Durgapur, 300 km from Calcutta. That, to city-bred ears, may sound like the back of beyond but, trust me, I spent the first 16 years of my life convinced it was the next best thing since Xanadu. To be fair to the place, back in the mid-70s and early-80s there was enough industrial excitement though not all of it productive to keep it buzzing. For its residents, of course, 'Dgp' (as it was affectionately addressed) was as good a city as any in the world with the possible exception, perhaps, of Calcutta.

Indeed, till I grew up and confronted my fair share of CBCs (city-bred cynics), I had no idea my salad days were something of an anthropological study. While one particularly well-heeled specimen insisted that my experiences 'out there' were the stuff of Jane Austen novels, others drooled over the familiar pincode 713206 calling it everything from quaint to quixotic.

The tragedy was that dear old Dgp had, by then, turned into a real boondocks which made any defence of the place tough if not impossible. But wait, there's more to my 'colony caper' than misty-eyed nostalgia. In the 16 years since I left Durgapur, I have come across what must surely be as formidable a network as the old boys one. My well-heeled friend calls it the 'D-Connection' and it has cropped up in the most unlikely places imaginable. From a couple of colleagues at the workplace to professional acquaintances and even stray encounters with complete strangers, the D-Connection has thrown up enough surprises to make me believe that the world is a small place, if not a small town.

Take the dinner invite from an out-of-town friend. He called to say he was bringing an old chum from college who, as luck would have it, turned out to be an ex-Dgp-ian. The rest of the evening our companions inspected the tableware in bemused silence as the conversation moved to Durgapur. The clubs. The schools. The school buses with the rather stern maxim 'Discipline, Sincerity' emblazoned on the sides. The gulmohur-lined avenues. The theatres. The marketplace...Or that other time when a pesky next door neighbour turned out to be an ardent Dgp-ian who made it his habit to drop in for some nostalgic networking almost every evening. Till his stint in the Capital came to an abrupt end much to my husband's relief. Of course, a couple of stray incidents do not a trend make. Indeed it took a fellow Dgp-ian to reinforce my faith in the trusted D-Connection. Like me, she came across the network in places as faraway as San Jose and LA. Because like the sepia-tinted school photograph, Dgp is much more than a memory. It's a time-warp that transports its former residents faster than Captain James D Kirk could say "Beam me up Scotty". Making a boon out of what's now the boondocks.